Dear Reader,

I'm Jo, a locc and I hope you ... a love story / crime drama set in the wilds of Yorkshire

(First Edition)

Orla Metcalfe has Run Away

Jo Priestley

If you could spare the time to do a rating or a review on Amazon, I would be so grateful

Copyright © Jo Priestley

All rights reserved.

Best wishes from Jo x

1

Other titles in the
Women of Old Yorkshire series
The Calling of Highbrook
The Strangers in Me
Little Robin

Dedication

With all my books I draw on the character traits of real people I've known past and present. Orla's story partly belongs to my great grandmother as she fled Ireland and remarried my great grandfather, creating a whole new life for herself in Yorkshire. Such a brave thing for a young woman to do, especially in the late 1800s.

Thank you again to Andrew for his support and editing skills and to Megan for adapting the cover from the artwork by the artist Alana Jordan.

Thank you to Ann and Tracey who review and critique my work and drive me forward to always do better.

Pip's tale is a change of direction in genre but as ever, a mother's love is explored as much as romantic love because both shape you as a person in different ways.

Chapter 1

Pip—1892

Maureen Davies is the font of all knowledge.

This is her own perception of course; I think she's just a tittle-tattling old busybody. She's never happier than when she's meddling in the affairs of others, but she plays her cards close to her chest. My mother would have called that sort of behaviour underhand.

If anyone mentions Mrs Davies's name, they generally tut or roll their eyes, so I don't think I'm the only one who thinks this. Anyway, she's in the perfect job for a busybody because you find everything out first at the corner shop.

She likes people to think she has a perfect life, but my mother said everybody, including Mrs Davies herself, knows 'her Walter' is seeing Nora Granger from the *Rose and Crown*. Nora's married too so I often wonder how and where they see each other. It all seems a bit grubby to me if I think about it, but I try not to.

"I don't know why she stays with him," my mother said once, "she must be blinkered or blinded by love's shining light. Only she knows what keeps her with a man who deceives her."

My mother often talked like that, all flowery as my father described it, but I loved to hear the words she used. I carried them around in my head and tried to use them without it seeming obvious. Sometimes I could tell my teachers were impressed, but then Evelyn said it made me sound like a show-off, so I stopped doing it. Now I just jot down the most special ones in a tiny notebook, so I don't forget them. From time to time, I leaf through the pages and picture my mother saying them in her soft, Irish accent. I keep those pictures alive in my mind for fear they might float away forever if I don't.

"How do you know Mrs Davies knows about Mrs Granger?" I asked my mother.

She stopped stirring the stew in the pot but didn't turn to look at me.

"Because I told her myself," she said flatly.

I couldn't have been more shocked. Why would she tell her I thought, why would she take it upon herself to tell Maureen Davies something which would change her life like that? I thought she couldn't care less about her.

My mother began stirring again, still with her back to me.

I had to ask; I just couldn't keep my mouth tight.
"Why did you tell her?"

My mouth dropped when she spun around, her face all twisted and pink. It made me take a step back as if that look could fly across the room and strike me.

"Because she'd a right to know what's going on behind her back. Your da told me and I told her so that's that! We'll say no more about it if you don't mind."

I didn't run from the room because I was rooted to the spot, but I waited until she'd turned back to the stove and then sloped silently out of the kitchen desperate not to draw attention to myself. My mother rarely got rankled as she called it, so it upset me more when she did.

"You after some baccy today for your da, Pip?" Mrs Davies asks now. Startled, a heat creeps up my face, certain she knows I've been thinking bad thoughts about her.

"Yes please, Mrs Davies," I say too loudly.

I brace myself for further questioning. If only the baccy was on the shelves I could just pay as quick as a flash and then scoot out the door. Today we're alone so I'm thankful for small mercies. It's even more uncomfortable when other customers are in the shop, and we have an audience.

"Your da alright then … and Liam?"

It's the same questions every time, said in the same way. I only come once a fortnight nowadays, but I think I dread this moment for at least a week before each visit. It reminds me. It reminds me my mother isn't with us anymore. Mrs Davies is only doing what she does with every customer, and it should be getting easier to cope with after three years.

"Yes, thank you, they're fine," I say.

I answer in the same dreary way every time as well. I can never say more even if I wanted because the words knot at the back of my tongue like a hairball. Watching Mrs Davies measure exactly twelve ounces of baccy takes time too, but a fortnight is a long time for my father to wait for the next batch. We don't venture here in between if we can help it.

While she works, she gives me a little update about her Ivy. Today she looks around to check nobody is with us, but the shop doorbell hasn't chimed to signal another customer has arrived, so I'm not sure why she would need to.

"Our Ivy's finished with Jack," she says, folding the brown paper bag to pass it over the counter, "she's not giving much away, but I think she's got her eye on somebody else."

Normally, the updates on Ivy are mundane—she'd bought a new hat, been to the theatre with Jack and such—but this little nugget means a response is required. Mrs Davies is looking at me, eyebrows hidden well underneath her greying fringe, and I know she's waiting for the response.

"Oh … I'm sorry to hear that, Mrs Davies."

I don't know if I've chosen the right one.

She shakes her head ever so slightly. Have I irritated her? Perhaps she was hoping I knew who the somebody else Ivy has her eye on is, but Ivy Davies is a stranger. Yes, we're similar age, went to the same school but I would never be in the know about what's happening in her daughter's life.

Ivy was never unkind to me, not like some, she was just indifferent towards me. I wasn't important enough to justify her time because as my father says, time is the biggest investment and most of us are miserly with it when it comes to unimportant things. I wasn't worthy of an investment and so she just acted as if I wasn't there. Eventually I realised it wasn't an act, I really wasn't there to the beautiful Ivy Davies.

Her shoulders rising towards her ears, Mrs Davies lets out a noise which could be mistaken for a sigh. I have irritated her then it seems. I try and think what to say, but she beats me to it.

"Well, Jack's heartbroken as you can imagine. They were thinking of getting married next year too, I'd been making enquiries at the *Travs*."

Why there? Nobody has a wedding reception at *The Traveller's Rest*. Then I remembered, the *Rose and Crown* is boycotted because of Nora Granger. This will have been a nasty tasting pill for her to swallow for so many reasons, Ivy being her only daughter especially. Having the do at the slightly shabby and run-down *Travs* would have been a right comedown. But she knows the villagers would never step out of Ackley for a wedding reception. Thinking of Nora suddenly makes my mother pop back into my mind. I want to get out of the shop, I feel hemmed in.

Bending my head into my basket I shuffle the shopping around and carefully place the bag of baccy on top. I need a moment to think.

"I suppose it's better that it happened now, so they don't need to call off the wedding," I say.

This time Mrs Davies nods and her narrow lips twitch into a gentle smile. This time I've said the right thing by the look of her, almost placated, like the thought had never occurred to her before. I hand over my money and she hands over my change for me to drop into my purse.

As she opens her mouth to speak again the doorbell sings and Mrs Davies greets Mrs Wilks. I expect I'll now become invisible as they chat about the weather turning fresh or some such dull subject.

But instead, Mrs Wilks shoots me a look as though I was the last person she would be expecting to see in here. Her cheeks blaze against her white wrinkled skin so vividly that I drop my eyes, I'm so unsettled by it. I glance over at Mrs Davies and tell her I must be on my way. She too doesn't know what to do about the look on her customer's face it seems.

"See you in a fortnight then," I say so quietly I doubt she heard me.

I nod at Mrs Wilks on my way past and sneak a peek at her face again. But she only stares straight through me, her head moving along in time with my footsteps, until I can feel her follow me out of the door. It's like she's seen a ghost and I'm it.

My father is waiting on the corner of Pawson Street sitting atop the cart attached to Bella, our new horse. He's puffing away on his pipe side on to me. He turns his head when he hears the bell.

The street is empty once Ginny Brownlow takes her pram inside the house opposite.

I wave at my father then pretend to check the *For Sale* notices in the window. This isn't unusual though I never buy anything because I make everything that I need myself. The two women in the shop think I'm on my way home already; they can't see me, but I can see them, and I was careful not to close the shop door properly. Mrs Wilks has already approached the counter, placing her basket on the floor as though she's set to stay awhile.

"I've had a right morning," Mrs Wilks says, looking over her shoulder, to make sure I haven't reappeared out of nowhere. I duck down instinctively though I'm well out of sight.

Mrs Davies rushes from behind the counter, "I can tell, Flo, you look like you've had a nasty turn," she says pushing a three-legged buffet reserved for the more elderly customers under her.

"Of all the people to be in here when I arrived, I couldn't believe it," Mrs Wilks says, going through her pockets. She finds a crumpled hankie and dabs her eyes.

My heart races and I'd like a stool to sit down on too. It's obvious this news will affect me and in an upsetting way.

"I didn't like her, not many did but that's not the point," Mrs Wilks says, her voice going in and out of her hankie as she speaks.

"Are you talking about who I think you are?"

Mrs Wilks only nods, blowing her nose loudly.

"Orla Metcalfe," Mrs Davies says leaning against the shop counter, "what is it now, hasn't she caused enough suffering for that family?"

Mrs Wilks sits perfectly still, staring straight ahead as though she can't find the words. I hear footsteps and my heart picks up speed. My father is heading my way, I've taken too long.

"Well, let's just say she won't be causing any more bother from now on, Maureen."

My father's footsteps are getting louder, but my feet just won't move.

"She's no more," Mrs Wilkes says, "they found her dead this morning. Cold as ice and stiff as a board she will be now."

I hear the words but I've no time to make sense of her statement properly. I can't risk my father finding out about my mother, not here, not now. Racing towards him I hold out my baskets, and he takes them to dangle like weighing scales from his arms to walk towards Bella and the cart. His cap is low over his eyes as always and his unlit pipe is sticking out of his top pocket.

When he asks me what was taking so long, I turn my head to wipe a tear with the sleeve of my mother's old coat.

Get a hold of yourself Pip, I think gulping down air quickly, he can't know our world has been tipped upside down. I'll have to talk to him and Liam when we get home before the rumours reach *Sunnyside*.

Will every lie send me to hell I wonder as I tell him I'd love to take a look at a second-hand dress I've seen for sale in the window.

Chapter 2
Jarvis—1892

"Come on … up with you my lad," ma says.

I'm startled from my sleep which is no way to start the day I think, rubbing my eyes. How I wish she wouldn't come in the room to wake me. I'm twenty-seven years old and it's now a step too far in my book. A man should have privacy and a mother should have boundaries with a grown son surely. She checks the collar of my shirt laying on the bed and tucks it under her arm for the wash basket along with my underwear. I've only just started to find her intrusions irritating. Thoughts of Ivy warm me when I wake, and I'd like a moment to myself without interruption. I groan, pulling the eiderdown up tighter under my chin.

"I'm not in until this afternoon, ma. I was hoping for an extra couple of hours to lie in this morning."

The bedroom window has frosted overnight, and clouds of moisture puff each word from my mouth. The bleak mid-winter is just around the corner.

"I've got your porridge all ready, Jarvis and I'll be beggared if I'm wasting it. I think you'll have to start leaving a note before you go to bed telling me when you're next in work. How am I supposed to know? I thought you'd be up and off this morning as usual. I don't know lad this new case seems to have taken over your life."

She's right it has taken over my life but is it any wonder?

"It is a murder case ma and there's never been one around here before," I say, sitting up in bed defeated, "well not in living memory at least."

There's no chance of more sleep and I'd rather my porridge didn't go to waste either.

She tuts as she walks to the door, grabbing my empty glass from the chest of drawers on her way.

"Some might say good riddance to bad rubbish, Jarvis. Good policemen working all the hours god sends trying to fathom out why one person would like to kill a woman who has… had a village full of enemies."

Sitting up I stretch my back and yawn, too tired to get worked up about the point she's making.

"Just because she wasn't popular doesn't mean she deserved to be murdered. It's still a crime."

"Wasn't popular—that's a kind way of putting it. She wasn't popular before she did what she did, but after that she was hated, nothing less. That poor little lass was devastated, never the same again I shouldn't wonder."

I understand what ma's saying, I do but I'm not here to sit in judgement of a person's character, I'm here to get to the bottom of the sorry tale.

What would dad do? Dad would kiss her cheek and tell her she was right. Then he'd work all hours God sent trying to find the murderer. He didn't rise to Chief Inspector by sitting on his hands and waiting for it to happen. Just one more step up the ladder, and I'll have matched him; a little personal goal achieved to tick off the list. I never really stopped to wonder why this was so important to me, but it is.

I'm lying to myself again I think swinging my legs out of bed onto the rug and shuffling for my house shoes. There's no list, this is the only goal I've had since I was thirteen years old. It's why I live at home, have never married, or even really courted a girl, not properly anyway until I started seeing Ivy.

Now I know my dream isn't only a pipe dream, it's achievable, almost in my grasp and solving this case will go a long way to earning me that extra pip on that shoulder slide of my dress uniform.

I shuffle over to the wash hand stand and splash cold water on my face from the jug and bowl, then throw on my trousers and grab a sparkling white shirt from the five hanging in a row in the wardrobe. Ma prides herself on my laundry as though her reputation as a proper mother depends on it. I'm not complaining, she looks after me well enough and she appears to enjoy it.

I never thought my hair my best feature—some may say it's mousy, but Ivy calls it tawny—the waves are thick, the pattern of them never changing unless it gets too long. I'm not a vain man but I've been known to turn a head or two in my time. I turned Ivy's head. I was in her mother's back room at the shop, having a cup of tea when she dropped it into the conversation that she'd called it off with Jack, the boy she'd been sweet on from school days. I can't be sure but there's always been a little tinkle in the back of my mind that there might have been a slight overlap between her finishing with Jack and starting up with me. I've no way of knowing for sure, and that's their business, I can only go on what she tells me.

As I bound down the stairs I wonder if Ivy will launder my shirts. Tucking into my lukewarm porridge I think I might need to make chief inspector if I have to get a woman in to do the chores. Ivy doesn't strike me as a washing and cleaning kind of girl and times have changed since my parents got married. But we might need to keep it quiet from ma as she would consider having a cleaner an indulgence. What am I doing thinking about marrying Ivy? I know she's pretty and I know she's keen, but marriage isn't a step to be taken lightly, not even when you know everyone else is holding their breath waiting for it to happen. That's not reason enough.

"Are you seeing Ivy any time soon?" ma asks, joining me at the table. It's as though she was reading my mind.

"I said we might go for a walk on Saturday, but I can't be too committal at the moment for obvious reasons."

"The woman's dead, she's not going anywhere. There's no rush surely and Ivy won't hang around forever," ma says, eyes wide and searching, her priority clear in her own mind. Her hand is resting under her double chin, and I look at it like I'm seeing it for the first time. I notice the cracked skin and the coarseness from her hard work. Ivy won't want hands like that. I study ma's tidy grey hair, and pristine pinafore and wonder where the woman went who lives in the photograph on the mantel. The one taken on the day she married dad with her shiny dark hair and slim figure, wearing her white, floaty dress.

"Ma, I haven't got this far to spoil my chances now by not putting my back into this investigation. It's a chance to prove myself and there'll not be another like it."

Pouring us both some fresh tea from the pot she sets her lips so tightly lines appear all around them. They will be desperate to burst open and I butter my toast and wait for it to happen. I don't have to wait long.

"Look, I'm your mother, so if I can't give you a few home truths then it's a poor do. Ivy is from good stock, she has breeding and to be crass, a bit of money behind her. If you mess this up, you'll have to settle for some *ordinary* lass who will bore you to tears in six months. I know my son and his wife is going to need something about her to carry him through a lifetime. I know you've worked hard, but timing can't always be perfect and somebody else might come along and poach her if you keep her dangling."

She's right of course, she generally is, but what she means by ordinary is more about lack of money than anything else. Ma is fond of money, but then as she points out often enough, we can't do much without it.

I cover her hand with mine and stare at her for a moment too long. She shifts in her seat.

"Well, the way I see it is that she's not the girl for me if she can be so easily swayed. I know you want the best for me, but there was no mention of love in your little speech."

Snatching her hand away, her eyes narrow. I sit back in my chair startled.

"Love; if only love was enough," she tuts scornfully and raises her eyes, "you need to like each other, respect each other, they're the most important things in a marriage."

Did she not love dad; was all my childhood a façade?

I must ask her.

Her eyes shine in the firelight, and she takes a long drink of tea. My toast lays half-eaten on my plate as I wait for her answer.

"Don't look like that," she says, "I did love your dad, I do love him. But it was luck more than anything else. I always thought I chose well and unlike many, he didn't turn into something else when we got married. Many a woman I've known has been swept off her feet by a man only to discover his other side when it was too late." She blows out a sigh as she pours herself a fresh cup of tea. "Look, you're pushing thirty Jarvis, you'll miss the boat if you're not careful and another one might never come along in this village of inopportunity. You know, I won't be around forever, and I'd like to see you settled."

She did love dad; that's a welcome relief. I suppose I always thought I'd find what they had together if I waited long enough, so if I found out it was based on a lie, I'd have nothing to hold onto anymore.

Has the boat already set sail without me? All those girls at school who showed an interest and went on to be shopgirls or millworkers, the ones I overlooked because I was only thinking of my career—have they been and gone already?

They might have but now there's Ivy. She might not be as capable as ma, as resilient as she is, but she's a catch. Beautiful people don't have the chance to become capable and resilient as there are too many other people falling over themselves to provide them with every whim. They're treated differently and I can't see as that's their fault.

"I'm glad we've had this chat," I say but ma looks unconvinced.

"You can make your mouth say owt I want to hear to get yourself off the hook, Jarvis Blackburn," she says, leaning across to smooth my forelock like she used to do when I was a kid.

Ma thinks I've struck gold with Ivy; my pals down at the station think so too and I bet dad would have done. Give it time and I will, I'm sure of it.

All I need to do is solve this case and then I'm all hers.

Chapter 3
Pip—1884

A white blanket of snow has covered the village and surrounding fields for forty-nine days now. I've kept a tally. I love snow but even I'm a bit sick of it now, I think as I kick an icy mound with the toe of my boot. My bonnet is pulled down almost to my nose as the brightness is stinging my eyes.

Evelyn, my sort of best friend, hasn't stopped coughing since we left school to walk home. That cold of hers is lingering but her mother will never give her time off, not for anything. My mother's the total opposite in that she finds any excuse not to send me to school. She says she's never happier than when we're all together.

"Let's stay home and finish that quilt we started," she'll say, or "lets read poetry and try and understand what it means."

It took me a long time to learn her favourite poets name by heart: *William Allingham,* that's too many 'ls' to say easily. He's her favourite mainly because he was born in County Donegal where she lived until she came to England but also because he wrote a beautiful poem about fairies. My mother likes mystical things as she calls them, things like fairies and the moon, and I like to listen to her reading poetry with her soft voice telling me what she thinks it means line by line. Her father was a private tutor for rich people until he died so their home was filled with books. I don't know many people who own one book, let alone have a shell full of them like us.

"Da was a wicked man, Pip," she told me once when I asked about him, "but the workings of his mind were fascinating. He could hold an audience in the palm of his hand, I saw it for myself at my uncle's wake one time. I don't remember what he was saying but I remember I couldn't take my eyes off everyone's faces as they listened to him speaking. They were enthralled, like he had them under a spell. When he finished talking, you could have heard a pin drop for six long seconds. I counted."

My father isn't like that. He doesn't talk a lot unless it's about a job he's doing, or telling my mother she shouldn't keep me at home now I have the opportunity to better myself and learn at school. She tells him I can learn more useful things about life at home with her, and he just shakes his head and smiles.

Sometimes I hide when he comes in for dinner from his workshop down the garden, so he doesn't know I'm at home. I can see him in blue overalls that are older than me, washing his hands before they settle around the table. When I'm hiding, I watch them through the tiny slit in the floorboards of my bedroom floor. My father always has his pencil tucked behind his ear, so now my brother Liam does too, it's like a uniform. He started as my father's apprentice only a year ago, so he's still breaking in his set of overalls my mother says.

"What're you having for tea?" Evelyn asks me now blowing her nose on a rag from her pocket. The colour of the tip of her nose matches her hair. Flaming fire my mother calls it and Evelyn blushes every time she mentions it so then her whole head looks like a fireball.

"Mine was nearly that colour once until I had scarlet fever and it lost its curl and went black as night," my mother said, "nobody recognised me, and I cried for two days. Black is such a common hair colour don't you think? Not like my little Pippin's hair here."

My father's hair is almost black whereas mine is so white that people always mention it. I don't really spend much time staring in the mirror as my mother says beauty is held within the soul and can't be seen through a looking glass.

"Potato and onion," I tell Evelyn, "As it's a Monday there might be a bit of leftover shin beef thrown in."

"Potatoes, potatoes, potatoes. Don't you ever eat owt else in your house?" she asks, rolling her eyes.

I can't help smiling. I want to explain it's an Irish thing; that my mother and her family ate potato every day when she was growing up, but Evelyn would only be bored listening to that. My mother cooks the same food and talks the same way as she always has, she's never lost her accent.

"Irish blood will forever course my veins," she sometimes tells me with a flamboyant gesture of her hand. She would do well on the stage.

A snowflake sticks to my eyelashes now, and I blink it away only for another one to do the same.

"Here it comes, it's a good job they sent us home early," Evelyn says, picking up her skirts to dash towards her house. Her voice is breathy from running when she shouts over her shoulder, "Are you sure you'll be alright from here, Pip, you can stay at ours if you like, my mother won't mind."

Her hand rests on the doorknob as she waits for my answer. It has always been the plan if the weather turned too bad and I was stuck in the village, but I can't stop at Evelyn's. Even though she says her mother wouldn't mind, she would because she doesn't like me, and I know it's because she doesn't like my mother. Her face looks a certain way when she asks questions about her as though she doesn't like the answer before I've said it. Sometimes I lie, I can't help it, but I think she knows.

"Does your mother miss living in Ireland, Pip?" she asked once.

If anyone else had asked me, I wouldn't have thought a thing but that look came over her face as I thought of what to say. The real answer is yes, she'd go back tomorrow but she can't, but Mrs Brookes would have been annoyed that my mother doesn't like Ackley.

"No, she's happy living here," I said, but my voice came out too high, even though I tried to control how it came out.

Then that annoyed look appeared anyway—the dark clouds rolling across her eyes before they narrowed and made me look away to stare out of the window.

My mother says everyone is born, raised, employed and married in Ackley and she's the first newcomer they've ever had aside from the odd farmhand travelling through. Mrs Brookes is like most of the women in the village, she says, and she won't be satisfied until she finds out everything there is to know about her life before in Ireland.

"People don't like it if they don't know the workings of you, it makes them suspicious," she told me, "They can't help it."

"No, that's alright, Ev," I call now, my feet still walking like I'm keen to get away, "I'll get a yomp on and I'll be home before the snow gets too deep, don't worry. Thanks though."

She waves but doesn't turn to look at me and I wonder if she's glad I refused her offer. A whole night or even more at Evelyn's; I pull my shawl tighter around me at the thought.

Except for the door colours, nearly every house in the village is the same as the next. Row upon row of them as far as you can see. Today it's quieter except for a few kids playing out, waiting for the snow to deepen so they can make snowmen. Our snowmen stay for longer because it's colder on the moor, so I really go to town on how big I make them and what they wear.

At the end of the street there are four bigger houses that stand apart just in front of the church. One of them is where Dr Johnson lives, another is the vicarage, and another belongs to Mr Sales, the millowner who lives there with his wife and nine children. The last one is exactly eighty-seven steps beyond, and it stands empty. It has an overgrown garden on all sides, and I always try and imagine who used to live here but I can't. I've heard it was royalty, but why would royalty live in Ackley when they could live in London? My father says it's more likely to have been some local bigwig, which is a far cry from a king or a queen.

Bunching my skirt, I tie it above my ankles and see my clogs are already getting sodden. It won't be the first or the last time I think, as I climb the first of eight stiles. I know this track like the back of my hand, my family having worn out the grass almost on our own. If I tuck under the overhanging branches of the trees by the drystone wall, I can keep myself from getting too wet for a about three of the four and a half miles home. The snow is settling already, but at least this will make it easier to walk and less slippery underfoot. Anyway, my father or Liam will come and meet me soon, they always do when the weathers bad. I laugh at the thought of the time my father fell when he was giving me a piggyback and I landed on top of him in a big heap.

"Don't you ever wish we lived in the village, da?" I asked him, pulling him up and brushing the snow from his coat and the bottom of his overalls.

"Never in a month of Sundays, love. I'd feel like a tiger in a cage, and I'd probably act like one. Come on, up you get Miss Pip," he said, heaving me onto his back again.

I didn't understand then, but I do now. They live cheek by jowl in the village my mother says, and she thinks that's an unhealthy way to live. I don't know if it's unhealthy or not, I just know I can only breathe properly when I turn off the road and on to the moorland track.

A wetness is clinging to me even through my shawl. It's coming down heavier now, but I'm caught betwixt home and Ackley, so I have little choice but to press on, Evelyn's mother's expression driving me forward. This is the first time I've felt worried about getting stuck because I've always been at home when we've had deep drifts before. Then I can't go to school for days. Once we were stuck for twenty-one whole days and I don't think I've ever been happier. My mother and I made an extra special quilt from old curtains and dresses I'd outgrown, and my father and Liam made a wooden dresser together.

"Well, I've been waiting long enough for one but I'm always at the back of the queue for furniture," my mother said, "the cobbler's children …"

"… never have shoes," we all said at the same time, then looked at each other and laughed.

During those long days, I didn't need to think about anything but fetching water and cooking stews. My mother told us stories when it got dark, some of them ghost stories so I had to wait for Liam to go up to bed as I was terrified. Somehow, we still loved to hear them which is odd when I think about it.

Where has everyone got to, I wonder now, shaking the snow from my shawl. I wish I hadn't bothered because placing it back around my shoulders is like sinking into a cold bath. My hands are going a funny shade of blue, and I'm even starting to think I should have taken Evelyn up on her offer to stay over. The cold must be getting to me.

"If you want to be happy and free from all fear, keep a horseshoe hung over the door," I sing quietly trying to keep my mind busy. My teeth are clattering together so loudly in my head and I'm getting so tired now to the point that I'm struggling to put one foot in front of the other. My legs are heavy and it's more difficult to raise my knees high with every step. Oh, da, please come quick with a dry shawl, there's only about three quarters of a mile to go but I need to sit down or climb on your back for a piggyback ride. I don't think I can carry on much further.

I start to cry. I can't help it, even though my mother would say the worst thing you can do in a crisis is panic, I'm panicking. Where are they? I can't see anything but white for miles but somehow, I still know where I am on the track.

I stop dead when my knees go, and I drop to the snow-covered ground with a small crunch. I roll my face out of the snow, but I couldn't get up even if I wanted to.

I lie so long I can feel myself going to sleep. Even when I hear a voice I've never heard before, I can't wake up, never mind get to my feet. I only know the voice isn't my father or Liam or even my mother.

"Christ, why didn't you stay in the village?" the voice asks.

The last thing I feel before I fall sound asleep is being lifted into the air but not for a piggyback ride.

Instead, I'm thrown over the man's shoulder so hard it hurts my stomach.

And all I can think of is the time I saw the farmer with a dead lamb slung over his shoulder, and it made me cry.

Chapter 4
Jarvis—1892

Ivy's mask has been slipping a bit. At first, she was in full agreement with me working extra hours, all supportive because she knew then it was essential.

"It won't be for long anyway Jarvis, we all know who killed her," she said.

Ivy might think she knows, I might even, but thinking is not the same as proving.

Now after ten days her support appears to be waning, and I'm trying to see it from her point of view. She wants me to call at her house for tea and cake this Saturday, but when a murder case is wheedling its way into most of your thoughts, visiting for tea and cake seems almost ridiculous.

"It will only take an hour of your precious time," she says her bottom lip curling downwards slightly so she looks like a petulant child. This is how I'm starting to think of her, especially when she talks to her mother. It makes me cringe.

Ma's words give me some comfort: "She's a special girl who deserves special attention," I remember her saying.

"I'll do my best to visit if I can get away. Will that be alright?" I ask, pulling her collar up towards her ears. Her dark red coat frames her cheeks, contrasting with her fair hair and complexion. Although she looks like a Christmas card, I know her mother will have spent an hour before opening the shop curling her hair. To be fair, the end result is always worth it.

I check we're alone in the bandstand though I'm certain we will be, there's only us daft enough to be out in this weather instead of in front of a blazing fire. My face draws nearer to hers.

"It'll have to do I suppose," she says stepping to one side.

Dad was often late home. His plate was pushed my way sometimes when it got so late his tea was on its way to being ruined. Ma might not have liked it, but I think she accepted it was all part of being a policeman's wife. Anything could happen anytime, and it didn't stop just because it was teatime. Dad didn't even have a murder to solve, surely this is my trump card for a while at least.

"He's evil that man," Ivy says sitting down on one of the long seats at the edge of the bandstand. Last time we were here the mill's brass band played for the village on a mud-cracking summer's day.

"Who?" I ask just to be sure we're not at crossed purposes. I barely hear her tut but it's there.

"Colin Pickersgill, who do you think?" she says.

I sigh at having to think about him yet again. Evil is a fair description of the man. He's obviously a bully and a brute and God only knows what Orla Metcalf saw in him.

"He has quite the reputation, yes," I say turning swiftly back to being a policeman.

This has started to niggle Ivy too. She expects me to tell her chapter and verse about what's going on with the case. If I did that, which I wouldn't, I don't think it would be very professional of me. Ma never …

I stop myself finishing the sentence. I'd do well not to keep comparing us with ma and dad because it keeps falling short.

"Quite the reputation," Ivy mocks, getting up from the freezing bench, "I don't think I saw Orla Metcalf without a mark on her face in all the time she was with him."

Ivy used to link arms with me when we were alone, but now she walks with her arms by her sides. I think about taking her hand then think better of it.

"If I can't talk about your work but you're there all the time then it's going to come between us don't you think?" she asks.

She's making a fair point I can't deny it.

Ivy's scent wafts my way. She always smells the same and I've seen the perfume in the bathroom. It looks the expensive kind in a fancy bottle. I'm not sure I would be able to run to it, I think as I study the skeleton trees lining the path to the road. I wish it were summertime again and I only had work to think about.

"Well at least can you tell me if you've spoken to Charlie now?" she asks, dabbing her pink nose with a handkerchief.

We've been out too long in the frost, and I don't want to talk about Charlie or anyone else in the frame for that matter.

"Let's change the subject," I say picking up pace. I'm cold but that's not why I'm rushing.

After more than a few steps I begin to wish I hadn't said it. I can't call a single thing to mind for us to talk about.

Glancing my way her brows are knotted waiting for me to speak and I can feel a blurt bubbling in my throat. It's out before I can stop it.

"Were you and Jack engaged?" I ask.

Her round eyes tell me this wasn't how she was expecting the conversation to turn.

"Why do you ask?"

There's a tiny smile about her lips showing me she likes this change of subject, but I don't. It's true, it has been on my mind on occasion but purely out of curiosity. Now the word has been said it has certain strings with it. You fool, Jarvis I think, you've gone and done it now, she'll go home and tell her mother she suspects I'm going to pop the question.

"It's only that you were seeing each other for a long time, so I wondered if he'd asked you to marry him."

Her hand was heading towards my arm, but she drops it quickly because she's still mad at me.

"Jack and I weren't suited. I always knew it but denied it to myself. He doesn't have any drive or ambition."

This doesn't really answer the question I asked but it tells me a lot. She wants a man who's confident, going places. To be fair to Jack, opportunities are limited at the mill. A wicked thought comes out of the blue: is it confidence or money she's after?

"Not like me then," I say with a cheeky smile.

I was hoping she might play along but she only shakes her head.

"You've got too much of it," she snaps.

I don't know if she means confidence or money, but I'm not put out, I'm only grateful I'm off the hook. She obviously doesn't think popping the question is on my mind now.

The houses draw nearer, the smoke from the chimney's mixing with autumn mist to create a veil around the neat rows. I suddenly realise I want to go home rather than call in at Ivy's house, but I tag along behind her down the ginnel, checking my watch. I've got about half an hour before I've to be back at the station.

Maureen appears from the shop at the front and clucks around us both making tea while Ivy warms her toes in the hearth. Her mother has always been so nice to me, and a pang of guilt appears that I can't bring myself to propose to Ivy when I know it's what they're both waiting for every time I visit.

I've only been seeing Ivy five minutes, so I don't understand how everybody else can be sure we're such a match when I'm not.

I sip my tea and think about Ivy as I listen to her mother chatting about the family at *Sunnyside* who have been left bereft and motherless after the murder.

"There's no point fishing for information," Ivy says shooting me a look, "he hasn't got much to tell us on the subject, have you, Jarvis?"

I feign a smile and reach for a biscuit.

Jack and I are the same it seems, we're both too much, too little, too this, too that for Ivy. She's like Goldilocks looking for someone just right.

But regardless of her mother and my mother's thoughts on the subject, I'm growing more unsure by the day now that someone is me.

Chapter 5
Pip—1888

We don't eat together around the table anymore, that hasn't happened for a long while. I don't know when it stopped but I wish I'd been paying attention so I could have made sure it didn't. It would be too awkward to bring up the subject now.

My mother and I eat alone, that's if she's bothering to eat, then my father and Liam come in later for the second sitting. I'm used to doing the shopping, cooking, cleaning and just about everything else that needs to be done nowadays. My mother can't help it; I know she'd help if she could, but she's not herself.

"I'm alright for any pie, love," she says from her chair by the fire.

She's like an ethereal figure haunting the cottage. My father was happy to pay and called Dr Johnson out but what's happening is affecting her mind not her body, the doctor told him.

"You don't have any pain, Mrs Metcalfe, so there's nothing I can treat I'm afraid. Perhaps I can prescribe a tonic to lift your spirits."

"But she's barely eating," my father said, his voice almost frantic like a man who was clinging on to his last shred of hope.

"Lack of appetite without other symptoms isn't seen as a cause for concern unless a person becomes weak or emaciated," he paused, "but then this would be seen as a psychological problem. I wonder if this perhaps is the start of it, only time will tell."

I heard all this through the gap in the planks of the kitchen ceiling. They were all in my mother and father's room upstairs and they thought I was outside. The staircase is in between the two bedrooms up there, and the other room is divided by a curtain for me and Liam. I consider us very lucky as some families have eight or nine to a room. They have coats on the bed as blankets whereas we at least have sheets and quilts. They're handmade but still.

I'd snuck back in and loitered by the door, ready to fly outside if I heard them coming downstairs. I too was worried sick about my mother, and I didn't want to be fed any half-truths after the doctor left.

Dr Johnson never came back. My father said he didn't want to risk any rumours starting and the rest of the world thinking my mother had gone mad. He thought the best approach would be to just sit tight and wait.

"With time and a bit of care she'll be back to her old self," he said.

That was over a year ago.

I don't say to my mother anything like, "Do you fancy just a bit of potato and gravy?" because it's wasting my breath. I'll plate her some up and she'll generally eat some food before bed. Just enough to keep her alive anyway.

Placing a fresh cup of tea on her side table—tea she drinks endlessly one cup after the other—I stroke her hair back from her face. She's still beautiful, and I don't think it's only me who would think it just because I love her. Her blue eyes tilt my way. Irish eyes, my father used to call them.

"I must tell you something, Pip," she whispers, "before the boys come in."

I hold my breath, my stomach warning me of bad news afoot. She's dying I think though surely, she can't know this for sure as the doctor hasn't diagnosed any illness. A tiny glimmer of hope stirs in my heart.

"What is it?" I ask, perching in my father's chair opposite, the tea towel still in my hand. My level voice is misleading, but a level voice is all I ever use, especially in my mother's presence.

She blows out her cheeks until they round, and I'm startled when a tear runs down one of them.

I start to get up and rush the few steps between us, but she holds up her hand.

Sitting back down heavily I twist the tea towel between my palms instead.

"Pip, if there was any other way, love, I would grab it with both hands, believe me. You're far more than a daughter, you're my best friend you know that and I … I wish it hadn't come to this."

My legs begin to quiver like the day I collapsed in the snow and when I woke up my mother and father were talking to each other downstairs, but I couldn't make out what they were saying. I only knew their tone of voice was different. They weren't exactly arguing, but their voices were loud whispers. I try so hard not to let this house have any secrets from me. I need to stay one step ahead to feel safe.

"I just can't find it in me to go on living like this," my mother says now.

I gasp and clamp a hand to my mouth. Is she wanting to take her own life; good god, does she want me to help her?

My safety net has failed me, my mother has disclosed a secret which is making me cry. I shall never feel safe again.

"No love, I'm sorry, I don't mean what you're thinking, it came out all wrong," she says, stretching across to pat my arm.

My mother's cold, bony fingers bring little comfort. Something tells me I'm not going to be soothed by what she's really trying to tell me.

She's struggling to find the right words to explain herself. I can only hear the fire and Bimble our cat purring gently as she washes herself.

My mother's face suddenly goes out of focus, then the room and I drop my head into my hands. I realise now exactly what she does mean.

"You're leaving," I say.

She doesn't nod or say a word, but I know I'm right. My mother wants to leave; my mother has wanted to leave here for a very long time.

The door opening brings my father and Liam in with the cold.

My father doesn't look over at us, he only kicks off his boots before washing his hands in the bowl of warm water waiting by the stove. My mother hasn't told him but perhaps he can sense what's been on her mind. Perhaps that's why he doesn't come in for tea with us anymore.

"What's up with you two, you look like you've lost a sixpence and found a penny?" Liam asks, warming his hands by the fire.

I'm careful not to look at my mother now when I say, "Oh, you know, women's stuff."

This is our tried and tested way of putting an end to a conversation we've found out over the years. My mother finds a shadow of a smile for her son, and he holds his grubby hands up telling us he'd rather not know any more. He's always getting into my ribs and making fun of me, but it's just his way. Rather this than watching his red-eyed stare when I woke after being brought in from the snowstorm. I didn't like that at all.

"Righto, enough said then. What's for tea, Pipsqueak?"

After washing his hands, he runs a hand through his mop of curly brown hair and sits opposite my father, knife and fork in hand. He knows that usually winds me up but today it doesn't. Famished from an afternoon in the workshop they both sit at the table waiting for their mutton pie whilst I breathe deeply but quietly through my nose to try and stem a flow of tears.

I can feel my mother's eyes on me as I trot around the room slicing pie and dishing up vegetables from the pans. I mustn't get ahead of myself— wherever she's going may only be temporary and perhaps I could persuade her to let me go with her. If I can do that then in time, I can surely persuade her to come home. She's so unwell but she might get back to her old self with a bit of time away.

I'd given up long ago trying to understand what caused this, but I suddenly remember Evelyn's mother talking about being too hot and feeling odd because she's at "that time of life." She's a similar age to my mother so perhaps she's at that time of life too. It's all I can think of.

I catch my father's eye as I put his steaming plate down in front of him on the table. When his hand touches mine so quickly and so lightly that only he and I notice, this time a pity seeps into my bones.

Liam distracts us saying, "You know, you'll make somebody a smashing little wife one day, Pip."

I don't care for once that there will be a punchline heading my way.

"That's if he can see past your ugly mush, of course."

It takes all the strength I can muster to push my tongue out playfully at my brother like always when he teases me. He grins, feeling satisfied with himself.

Oh, Liam I think, at this moment I envy your blissful ignorance of the situation. Was that me only moments ago?

I feel aged.

Chapter 6
Pip—1888

"Bedtime, da," I say, throwing the tealeaves on the fire to dampen it.

He gets to his feet obediently and the sadness gets a hold of me, as it seems to do so often. It's like I've become the parent, life's all skew whiff nowadays.

Liam turned in an hour or so ago. He tends to go out most nights as he's started courting Sarah Morton. She works at the mill and her father was made up to supervisor there not long back, so he had a couple of pieces of furniture made. The family have done up the big, old house in the village, the one I used to make up stories about when I was young. Liam met Sarah when he delivered the chest of drawers and washstand to her house on the cart. My father never goes in the village now, but I'll have to get him to take me to the shop instead of Liam before too long. There's a world of difference between living a quiet life and being reclusive.

Business has never been so good; people are falling over themselves to give him work. Nothing fancy as they can't afford it really, but everybody needs furniture, and my father has always undercharged. His skill is way beyond a cabinet maker, he's a master craftsman I'd say, but he only takes what he needs from his customers.

They feel sorry for him that's why he has so much work but at least it keeps him busy.

"Thanks, love," he says when I place one of the lighted candles from the mantle in his hand.

Following him up the stairs I kiss his cheek before he goes into his room, and he draws me to him briefly. This simple gesture of affection always makes me want to cry so I'm glad to turn and head into my half of the bedroom opposite his.

Liam is snoring softly behind the curtain when I go in. I like to go to bed as late as possible as my father doesn't sleep, I know he doesn't. The fire's nearly out but the room's still toasty as I slide into the cool sheets and rub my legs up and down to warm them up.

This is the worst part of my day, though I'd say it's getting better than it was. For two weeks or more after my mother left, I cried myself quietly to sleep. I could hear the occasional soft snivel behind the curtain, so I knew Liam was doing the same. He took it bad because at least we had some warning, whereas he had a belt from the side that knocked him clean off his feet.

It might have been better to warn Liam but right up until the very last minute, I didn't believe my mother would actually do it, I didn't think she could actually leave us.

I try not to let my mind go to that day, but it's been three months and I still can't help reliving it every night when my head hits the pillow.

The day after she told me she had to leave, I was still hopeful I could go with her, and this thought kept me going. I was desperate and had so many questions, but instead I ended up pretending we never had the conversation. I put the tea on while she had a lie down, soothed by the familiar routine, almost believing she'd come downstairs and sit by the fire like any other day.

But then when I went upstairs to check on her, I had a cruel reminder. As I went in, she was trying to hide a tatty carpetbag which I'd never seen before under the bed. I knew straight away what it was for and what she'd been doing.

She held out her arms and as tempted as I was to run to her and sob into her skirts something stopped me.

"Pip, love," she said, "I could just have gone when you were at the shops, I thought of doing that many times, but I couldn't do it in the end. I couldn't just leave a note and disappear. This way is hard I know but it's the lesser of two evils. At least I hope so.

I'm still not sure if it is.

"Does da know?" I asked, sitting on his side of the bed with my back to her.

"Yes, of course," she said but she didn't elaborate, so I wasn't sure how much he really knew, "now I must tell Liam tonight but ... but I'm not sure if I can do it."

Something strange happened, something which had never happened before with my mother: I felt angry towards her.

"So, you can tell da and me but telling Liam is too hard. Why is he so special?"

Turning around she put her hand gently on my back, but I shrugged it off, suddenly unable to bear her touch. But then the guilt flooded me, making me run around the bed to push my face into her lap like I wanted all along.

"I'm sorry, mam, I'm so sorry. Please, just let me go with you. If you're going back to Ireland I can come. You don't have to go forever, only until you feel stronger. If it's because you don't love da anymore, you told me absence makes the heart grow fonder. You might grow to love him again if you have some time apart."

A strange gurgle sounded in her throat as she lifted my head up, holding her fingers under my chin, her thumbs on my cheeks. She looked so ill. Is she going away to die, I thought? I couldn't understand what had happened when I thought I noticed everything.

"Pip, listen to me now and listen well, you need to be a grown-up about this, or you'll not get through it. I love your da, I will love your da for the rest of my days. If it was as simple as that I'd stay, if only for you and Liam. You're young, there's so much you can't understand, and I wouldn't want you to. I'd like to take you all with me, but I can't … I just can't!"

Burrowing her face into my hair she wept like I'd never heard anyone weep before. Is she having a breakdown, I wondered, has she gone mad and will need to be taken away anyway? The sound and the depth of her despair terrified me.

Her tears were dripping down my back, wetting my thin dress. I didn't pull away until she stopped crying then wiped her face on her skirt with one arm still around my shoulders. We laid side by side then on the top of her bed for a while in silence until we heard the outside door go and I jumped up to go downstairs.

That night my father sloped off to bed and as he left to go upstairs, I wanted to yell at him, "Do something, da, for pity's sake do something, say something. You can stop her I know you can."

But I didn't say anything. She'd been in the state she was in for more than a year and I suddenly realised there would have been untold whispered conversations between them as man and wife. Private conversations not fit for their children's ears.

My mother stayed downstairs saying she had stomach pain the same as the night before and I laid in bed waiting for her to come up and tell Liam.

She never did.

The next morning, when my father went out to the workshop, I followed him. I heard my mother close the door after us, so Liam was trapped inside. He couldn't get out so he had to listen to what she told him, and he wouldn't be able to change her mind though he wouldn't know it then, like I hadn't known it.

My father had just finished an order of a side table. It looked like Liam had started staining and polishing it the night before, so I took up the rag and carried on where he'd left off. By the time I'd finished it was the colour of honey and my father said I could have a job.

Liam wasn't as quiet about it all as I was, but by then my mother already had one foot out of the door. He yelled at her, calling her horrible names until my father went out to tell him to pack it in.

I watched Liam from the open door of the workshop. He shrugged my father's hand away from his shoulder then he ran down the hill to throw himself into my arms, so I nearly fell backwards. He sobbed like when he was little, and he'd cut his finger or grazed his knee, and my mother was the only one who could shut him up squalling.

When my father reappeared, I knew she'd left by then and my hope of her ever returning was all but gone. I realised she would never have caused us such pain if her intention was to come back.

And when Liam ran out a minute or two later yelling her name and she'd already disappeared, for a split second I wished she had died, so I would be able to make sense of it.

So, help me, I can never forgive myself for it, but I did.

Chapter 7
1892- Jarvis

This isn't his first time in a police station, he's far too at home. Sometimes our 'visitors' as we refer to them have eyes like saucers jumping at their own shadow—they're the destitute ones who've been forced to steal some food—some complain too much about lack of privacy and facilities, and others treat it all like a mild inconvenience. Bradley Foster falls into the latter category.

He ate all his foul-smelling food in the cell this morning, every last dollop, then washed it down with tea the colour of tar and no milk. Unlike his cellmates, the two lairy drunks fighting about something and nothing in the *Travs,* he looks remarkably fresh for a night on the tiles. He's now sitting at the table in our one and only interview room with a bored expression which hasn't shifted since yesterday. It's his second day of questioning, but today is different to yesterday. Today a single item has been found at the scene which may or may not be evidence. It's waiting on a tray wrapped in a pristine white cotton bag and labelled *Case No: 5327/Item 01* in writing I don't recognise probably because there are one or two unfamiliar faces appearing at the station as this is a murder enquiry. The item has only just been located because it had rolled under the dresser and caught between the floorboards of the cottage Foster shared with Orla Metcalfe. I may not be sure of its significance yet, but I'm certainly interested in his reaction when it's presented to him. I'm going on instinct here and to be honest, I have nothing else to go on. A big, fat nowt as dad would have said.

Foster speaks very little, playing for time with his responses so he doesn't trip himself up is my guess. It's all a game and one in which he's clearly an expert.

Not much is known of him other than he's a homewrecker according to everyone in the village or would that title befit Orla Metcalfe better? Either way, he came, he worked on the farm, he lived in a barn with the farmer's permission and kept himself to himself for long enough. The village didn't know of his existence until the scandal broke which is nothing short of a miracle around these parts. Maureen found all this out from the gossip train and kept everybody up to speed. If anything happened big or small in Ackley, Maureen was always my first port of call before I started seeing Ivy. I'd go in the back way for a cuppa and a chat and just listen as she nipped in and out between customers. She loved it when I took down a note, like she was solving the crime and in a way she was. She's always liked me and it's fair to say I like her too; I've known her since I was a kid and she'd pop a couple of extra pieces of toffee in my paper bag and wink. You don't forget things like that.

"I bet you're dying to find out what's under there, aren't you?" I ask Foster now, nodding towards the piece of cloth.

Foster's lips twitch upwards so slightly it can hardly be called a smile but that's what it is, a sardonic smile. I'm in no hurry to uncover my findings for him, he can wait a bit longer.

"Do you miss your—what shall we call her—your mistress?" I ask.

I'm getting sick of him toying with me. He's not too much older than I am but he looks down on me like I'm some wet behind the ears whippersnapper without any proper policework under my belt. He knows what to do, or what not to do to give us the run-around, so I'll have to try a different tack.

"The silent treatment won't work here, you know. It might have worked in the other nicks you've frequented but not here. You need to prove you didn't do what you did, in this case murdering Orla Metcalf and you can't do that without opening your mouth wider."

He holds my gaze, so I begin to sweat under my collar. I hate this windowless room it seems to suck all the air out.

Sgt Rogers, better known as Rodge, is writing everything down as we speak. He's gone through some pencils since yesterday noting down what I've said, but the prime suspect's words are limited to a few lines.

Chief Inspector Douglas went home for some sleep late last night after a tiring day trying to break Foster down. I was worn out too but then I'm nearly twenty years younger than him, so I have an advantage.

Foster's expression remains impassive. I'd like to rattle him in some way to get some reaction, any reaction will do. Is he the nasty piece of work everybody says he is I wonder. Orla did appear with bruises at the shop often, just like Ivy said, but then so do half the women in Ackley and their husbands aren't tarred with the same brush. No, the villagers don't know the first thing about him, so they can hardly sit as judge and jury.

I let out a long breath, but I make sure its silent.

"Do you miss her?" I ask again, this time trying to put a little note of empathy in my tone. There's a long pause which may seem to him for effect but really, it's while I think what to say next.

"What do you think?" he asks eventually, his voice low, the question rhetorical.

I try to keep my face as expressionless as his. This is good, this is progress. His response may be surly and useless, but at least I've discovered a chink in his armour, a way in.

"I think Mrs Metcalfe must have thought a lot about you to walk away from her family like she did. You must have been close. It's understandable that you would miss her, in fact it's only right."

I'm awkward talking about emotions especially to this cold blood but I need him to get onboard. Does he know this is my very first murder investigation I wonder. I have a feeling he will be able to smell my anxiety from a mile away.

His grey/brown hair is thinning a bit at the widow's peak but other than that he's quite good-looking. I can see why Orla was so taken with his brooding looks compared to Charlie's honest-as-the-day-is-long face. I would imagine Foster has had plenty of attention from the opposite sex.

"Now you come to mention it, will you be questioning Charlie Metcalfe?" he asks now, one eyebrow tilted slightly, "he's got more reasons than me if we're counting."

He's so cocksure of himself, with his mocking tone. His accent isn't from round here, but I'd say it's still Yorkshire. He said yesterday he's from the south and that took about two hours to establish with him going around the houses. It will all be followed up in due course, I'll not leave any stone unturned.

I ignore his question, but that won't come as a shock him to him.

"So, you said you came home from the *Travs* and Orla was there, dead on the bed. As far as you're concerned, she could have been there for hours as you went out about seven o'clock, you said. When we got there, a chair was overturned, and a clock was on the floor like somebody had done a poor job at making it look like there'd been a scuffle of some sort."

He shrugs his shoulders once as I stare at him waiting for a response.

"I didn't need to raise the alarm you know; I knew what path it would take us down," he says.

He's right he didn't, but then it could be a double bluff. He's astute enough to think of it I can tell already. I knot my hands at the back of my neck and lean into them.

"The thing is, we know you were at the *Travs* as there were plenty of people who saw you, but to be honest you could have murdered Orla before you left or after you got home. The general consensus is you were chattier than usual which is odd. Did you want to make sure people remembered you were there all night is the question I keep asking myself."

"Huh, I wouldn't say chattier," Foster says flatly, "I don't remember talking to anybody all night after getting my pint."

He's warming up a bit, so I decide to keep tugging at threads here and there. Tell a few lies and get him to defend them, it's all part of the training, some of which came from my own father.

"You'd only just started going in the pub apparently. This gives you a nice little alibi don't you think?"

He shakes his head but doesn't speak. He'd been going in the *Travs* for about six weeks according to the landlord, so hardly a new habit but as he's been around here five years or so perhaps it is. I'm getting tired. I think it's time to show him my cards.

Pulling the string on the white evidence bag I leave the item inside undercover, only placing the label by its side. Foster briefly glances down at it before he continues boring into my face with his eyes. There's nothing but blank whitewashed walls in this room with a table and the three chairs we're sitting on so there's little else to look at. I can't let him get to me.

"This is what we found," I say. I don't elaborate. I doubt it will be much use to the investigation as it's not a weapon but 'no stone left unturned' is the motto of the hour.

I tip the bag slightly and watch as the half-used yellow pencil rolls out and sits between us on the desk. Foster's eyes lower again after a second or two, but this time something different happens, this time when he looks at me, his smile is unmistakable. A wide grin is splitting his face from ear to ear making him look almost sinister.

I immediately wonder if he's just amused by the convoluted drama that I'm creating in unveiling my one shred of possible evidence.

Then a low chuckle escapes him, so I look up quickly. The sound floating around the quiet room disturbs me. I would not like to get on the wrong side of this man.

"You know what that is don't you?" Foster says now, his smile widening even further.

I've no idea so I can only remain quiet. It's a fair assumption this cocky little sod knows something I don't, and he's set to enlighten me whether I like it or not.

"That's a carpenter's pencil you've got there," he says, "I'm no carpenter, so if I were you, I'd get my boots on and scarper up to Charlie Metcalfe's place. I can't imagine how that got in our house, but you're barking up the wrong tree here."

I'm fighting the urge to snatch it from the table and take a closer look, though I know I'll not see anything I haven't seen before.

A carpenter's pencil, how the hell would I know that? Christ, how I'd like to lunge across the table and wipe that smile from Bradley Foster's face right now.

He opens his eyes wide, the smile still sitting behind them telling me how much fun he's having.

"Will it be alright for me to go now then … *Inspector*?"

Chapter 8
Pip - 1888

"I've got something to tell you," my father says, putting his knife and fork down on top of his half-eaten shepherd's pie.

It's funny when somebody says those words. It's generally life-altering and you know immediately from the person's face which way the hammer is going to swing. This isn't good news. I lock hands with Liam under the table. His palm is sweating ... or is it mine?

"I'll have to tell you before somebody else does," he pauses, picking his fork up to fiddle with it, "it's your mother, she's ... she's not living far from here."

I drop Liam's hand and cover my mouth with both hands. Oh, joy of joys, she didn't go back to Ireland. Perhaps she's coming home. My hands still on my mouth I look between da and Liam whose brow is furrowed with confusion. Come on, Liam, catch up with me, I think.

My father drops his fork on his plate and pulls one of my hands away from my face to hold it.

"Pip, love, she's not coming home, I'd like to give you the good news that she is, but she isn't. I haven't been entirely honest with you because I secretly still hoped she might come home to us, the same as you did. Before she left, she told me she'd like to see you if you'd agree, and I kept quiet about it. The thing is you might not want to see her after what I have to tell you. But we all must accept she's left here for good, me included."

"Of course, we'll see her, da," Liam says quickly, "where is she?"

Slumping in his chair, my father rubs his whiskery chin, so I hear the rasp.

"Hold your horses, lad, I need to put you in the picture first, then I'll tell you."

"Is she in hospital?" I ask suddenly, "She was so ill, wasn't she; has she gone to the madhouse for treatment?"

He shakes his head, tightening his grip on my hand.

"No, kids listen to me, this isn't what you want to hear. Yes, you can see your mother but she's not living…not living on her own."

I swallow hard. Not living on her own, what does he mean? Whatever news you have, just get on with it da, I think.

"Look, feeding us titbits of information is torture, da. Start from the beginning and just tell us properly," I say, glancing at Liam. His face is stiff and grey, and he nods at me in agreement.

My father gets up to shuffle the few steps to the fire and takes a pipe from the rack on the mantle. To my mind they've never been used, but he goes to a drawer of the dresser and takes out a leather pouch to fill the pipe with tobacco. It's the pipe with a man's face and flat cap on it and I wonder if he carved it himself, but I don't ask because I really don't care.

After lighting the pipe, he sits back in his chair. He looks like an old man; I forget he's a lot older than my mother because I've never really looked at him nor Liam properly for ages. Their obvious pain seeps into my heart now like blood into a bandage, their wounds clearly on show for me to see all the time.

I turn round in my seat to face my father, and Liam makes a quarter turn to do the same. He's not looking at us, only staring glassy eyed straight ahead at my mother's empty seat.

"It's been hard knowing what and how much to share with you both. You're on the cusp of adulthood but not quite there yet. Perhaps all this has pushed you over the line, but you're still youngsters."

Liam and I steal a glance at each other. He's only fifteen months younger than me but he's been mollycoddled by my mother and me. Now I suddenly realise he's grown into a man. Would this have happened if my mother had still been here, I can't help but wonder.

The smoke from my father's pipe wisps above his head to disappear behind the beams of the ceiling. He's not really with us, he's wandered off to yesteryear.

"When I met your mother, she'd come over from Ireland and she was working at the mill covering for someone who'd just had a bairn. She was going on to the next town to find work but when I met her, I was changed. Yes, we all know she was beautiful, but it was the way she spoke to me. Because I don't talk much, people can sometimes think I'm a bit simple or I don't have owt much to say, but she didn't. Your mother didn't. She knew I only spoke when it was worth saying and I like listening more than talking. You're a bit like that, Pip, so you understand." He pauses, and I nod because I do understand. "She was lodging with

Ginny Brownlow's mother, but she was never in the house much. She'd come up here to *Sunnyside* and spend hours looking at the ancient battle graves. She'd make up stories about the people and make me laugh. She was a bit, well quite a bit younger but she was a woman not a girl. It was lonely up here after Peggy and Isaac died …" he stops talking and takes a long drag on his pipe.

Peggy was his first wife who died giving birth to their son, our brother, Isaac who also didn't survive. It was never a secret as far as I know, but it was my mother who told us about it and da has never mentioned them before. His expression is too sad, and my chest feels tight.

"Well, the rest is history," he says coming back to us, "your mother and me married and not long after we had you, Pip and then you, Liam. Your mother was, is a different kind of person, you've no doubt gathered this over the years. She's quite a spiritual person as I think of her, and the highs and lows of life affect her deeply. She was struggling as you know," he looks at us then starts saying something much louder as though the words are bursting out of his mouth, "she was struggling so much because she fell in love with somebody else."

From the corner of my eye, I see Liam's head twist my way like his neck is on spring. I don't look at him because I'm trying to understand what my father can possibly mean. I think he said my mother loves somebody else; that she left us to go live with somebody else and not very far away by the sound of it. My mother would never do that, not to us. Even if she

56

could do it to our father, she wouldn't be able to do it to Liam and me.

"My mother wouldn't do that to us, da," I say the words in my head out loud.

I speak for both of us as Liam has lost his voice, all the stuffing knocked out of him.

Putting his pipe on the hearth my father leans forward, his elbows on his thighs to give us his full attention.

"You both saw the state she was in when she left, no more than six stone wet through, barely getting a wink of sleep. It was making her ill, mentally unstable. She didn't want it to be, but it was, she couldn't help it."

I'm startled when Liam jumps up from the table scraping his chair across the stone flags and running his hands frantically through his hair, so it stands on end.

"How can you defend her for god's sake, da. Have some self-respect, she's made a fool out of you more than any of us. If what you're saying is true, I don't want to see her, I'll never see her again as long as I live. A mother shouldn't leave her children, not ever, not under any circumstances."

He charges past me and up the stairs then I hear the creak of the bed as he sits down heavily on the mattress. I want to go to him, but I want to stay with my father, I don't know who needs me the most in this moment.

My father's eyes are glossy in the candlelight as he looks at me. I've never seen him cry, not even after my mother left and it sends me flying to his side.

"It's alright, da, it's alright," I say as I slide my arms around his neck.

"Don't hate her, love," he says in a broken voice, "I don't hate her, I never could."

I'm crying with him because I can only imagine the pain of having someone that you love like he did my mother slip through your finger's day by day. I push my face deeper into his neck at the terrible thought.

My father needn't worry because I don't hate her either.

Though I wish with all my heart that I could.

Chapter 9
1892 - Jarvis

In all my life, even before joining the police I've never ventured this far on the moors. Why on earth would I need to? When we played out as a kid it was in the woods by the mill or on the street—the moors were a vast eyrie place, full of folklore to deter us. I don't think any of it was based on fact come to think of it, but it stopped us kids from straying too far.

The villagers thought that when Orla Metcalf took up with Bradley Foster it was because the isolated life that she lived here had sent her mad. Ma did too and she said it was only to be expected when people lived like animals in the wilderness.

I understand why there are such stories because this place *is* like a wilderness, an unforgiving world in wintertime by the look of it. How the Metcalfe kids used to walk this far is beyond me, no wonder they weren't in school so much of the time.

They're not kids anymore, but they still choose to live in the back of beyond. I see Liam knocking about the village more now he's engaged to Sarah Morton from the mill, but I can't remember the last time I saw Pip face to face.

The snow cleared last week but the flurries returned a couple of days ago. It's coming down now, but my boots are up to the job so far.

I pull my collar up a bit higher and think of Foster, he's tucked himself up nicely in a corner of my mind. I can't lie, he's managed to get under my skin just the way he wanted.

Ivy's been a bit off with me as I didn't go for tea at the weekend. I was swamped with meetings and reports, but mainly I've been obsessing about yon fella, I can't help it.

I knocked on Ivy's door on my way to the station to tell her. She had my favourite dress on, the green one. I told her it suited her, and I immediately felt bad that she must have been thinking about me when she picked it.

"My mother baked a cake especially, Jarvis," she said, "Lemon and sultana, your favourite too."

"I'm sorry," I told her, "But I did say I'd only try my best to make it if I could. Your ma shouldn't have gone to any trouble for me."

What I really wanted to say was, "I've got bigger things to worry about at the minute Ivy, than lemon and sultana cake, and you should know it," but it wasn't Ivy's fault. She didn't murder anybody.

"You know, I'm beginning to think I'm playing second fiddle. What happens if there's another murder tomorrow, next month? I don't think I'm cut out to be second fiddle, I don't think you should want me to be one either," she said sullenly.

"When this is over, I'll have more time for you. This is the first murder in the village in forever, so I should think we're safe on that front."

She sniffed and shook her head telling me she'd heard enough.

"Well, you'd better get on with it then. See you if and when you nail that vile man to the post," she said, shutting the door in my face with a little too much force.

Her parting shot hit a raw nerve. If only I could nail him Ivy, it would give me the greatest pleasure and a good night's sleep I thought, mounting my bike to head to the station.

I know I shouldn't let him win, but just thinking about that 'you can't touch me' expression he wears on his face and his high and mighty manner makes me want to prove he killed Orla all the more.

But then he's right, why would a little yellow carpenter's pencil be at the scene of the crime? It was hidden from view admittedly, but why *would* it be there? I suppose Orla could have taken one when she left, but it's such an odd thing to pack when you're leaving your husband and kids for your lover.

What's this on the horizon? Surely it must be *Sunnyside* cottage now I've walked to what seems like the end of the earth. I pick up speed at the welcome sight of it. It's actually quite pretty I realise as I draw closer, a little house made of stone with a drystone wall surrounding it. I've done my homework and I know that Charlie Metcalfe built it and pays a peppercorn rent for the small piece of land to old man Nicholls who owns this stretch of moorland. The family has been here a long time and he looks after it well I can see.

Ma has a couple of pieces of Charlie's work at home. He's a gifted craftsman there's no doubt about it and she takes a pride in polishing the table and dresser every week. I only found out he made them when I told her I was coming here. I'd never really thought about Charlie Metcalfe until a few days ago and now he and Foster are all I think about. I'll see how it goes after we have a little chat, but I think he'll have to come back to the station with me. Charlie has certainly got motive enough and now with that darn pencil ...

I need to catch my breath, so I lean against the solid wall to take in the scene. Before today if I'd been asked to describe *Sunnyside*, I think I would have imagined a tiny rundown cottage. It's tiny alright but it's a sight for sore eyes in the middle of nowhere, with smoke curling from the chimney and tidy little cottage garden out front.

I can't wait to get out of this freezing cold. Hopefully they'll put the kettle on for me even though I won't be the most welcome visitor to ever land on their doorstep.

Charlie suddenly appears from somewhere behind the cottage, hands in the pockets of his overalls, looking up at the falling snow. He sets off to go inside then spots me, taking his hands out of his pockets and waiting.

Stopping at the gate I put my hand up and he follows suit. He's a pleasant chap from what I know of him. I don't think we've exchanged more than a few words before today but like the wall he built he seems the strong, solid type.

"Can I have a word, Mr Metcalfe," I shout from the gate, somehow wanting permission to enter his land even though I've every right to be here.

He nods saying, "Come on in the gate, lad, erm … inspector. I've been expecting you."

I walk down the path, but we don't shake hands to greet each other. This isn't a social call when all said and done, and he knows it as well as I do.

"Are you mad coming out in this weather?" he says attempting a small laugh.

Looking back, I see the view he sees every day of his life and my jaw hangs at the sight of the rolling snow-covered moors, a ridge line on the horizon hiding the view into the valley and on to Ackley. I've no time for admiring the view, the snows coming down a bit heavier, so I better get on with what I need to do.

"Come inside," he says, and I follow behind him to what I imagine is the one and only door to the cottage. He looks like he made it too along with the gate and probably every other item of wood furniture inside I should imagine.

The warmth hits me as he opens it to go in and I take off my cap to shake the snow from the peak. I don't want to trail water inside with me, ma brought me up well.

"Pip, we have a visitor," he says, "Inspector Blackburn's come to have a chat with me. A hot brew wouldn't go amiss if you don't mind, love."

Moving to one side to allow me entry my eyes adjust from the brightness of the snow to the cosy hue of the cottage inside.

Pip stops in her tracks with the kettle in her hand, stopping to give me a polite nod without a smile.

Suddenly my eyes could not be more focused. I must try my best to stop my bottom lip dropping for the second time in as many minutes.

I must have missed it happening when I was busy chasing my dream of walking in my father's big shoes. But when did that scraggy little duckling I once knew, transform into the most beautiful swan of the flock?

Chapter 10
1889 - Pip

For the first time in I don't know how long my father is going with Liam on the cart to the village. He needs a lift with the table and chairs they're delivering to Ginny Brownlow's house.

Strangely, it's the first time I've been alone at *Sunnyside* in my entire life; the thought only just occurring to me. Standing at the window I watch them trot down the track with Bella pulling the cart. I swallow a couple of times. They're my whole world now, and if I lose them, I will lose everything including this cottage, my safe haven.

I turn swiftly from the window and pull my mind away from that awful thought.

"Come on Phillipa," I say out loud, "you've been waiting for this moment for long enough. Stop your maudlin thoughts and get your skates on."

I'll never make it back in time before they both return but I've thought of this already—I'll just have to say I've been into the woods for mushrooms and make sure I remember to pick some on my way back. I take one of my father's pencils and write a short note to that effect, putting the paper in the centre of the table. This is the only place I can be sure they will see it as those two never look further than the end of their noses.

Grabbing my basket from the hook by the door, I put my shawl inside. The weather's warm, but it can change in an instant out here. I've learned the hard way over the years never to leave the house without it.

There are some late flowering sweet peas growing by the door and I break a handful of stems as I pass. Their powerful scent brings back memories I'd rather forget but I can't turn up empty handed it wouldn't be right.

Under different circumstances it would be a pleasant walk this afternoon. This isn't a path I've needed to travel far down before so if my mind wasn't elsewhere there'd be plenty to look at. I try to calm my fluttering thoughts by listening to the lark's trill and chur as they take flight from the heather, but I can't listen for long.

When I picture my mother, my stomach does a somersault and then I think of my father and Liam, and it flips back again. Back and forth it goes now, worse than it's ever been. Well, since the day she left anyway.

My father would be glad I'm going to see her I hope but Liam will never forgive me if he finds out. He's raw and can't get past the thought of her being with somebody else. I understand you Liam I think, you often forget I'm the one who knows exactly how you feel.

Have I got past it? No, but then I want to see my mother more than anything else in the world, more than upsetting my brother even. She was so poorly when she left. How will I feel if she looks better; will I be glad or resentful? Oh, that's far too complicated a question to answer—a bit of both, I should imagine.

Veering down the banking I cross the steppingstones at Lilla Beck, concentrating hard so I don't fall in and get swept away. My skirts are wet as I climb back up the banking on the other side, but they'll soon dry off in this weather.

I can see the barn in the distance, quite far away from the farmhouse by the look of it. With my hand shielding my eyes I take it in. Is that really where's she's been living almost a year? A barn is meant for animals, so the windows are too high and too small and there's a barn door which is slid open and leaning against the wall.

I'm trying to swallow down my own heartbeat as I creep nearer, wondering if either of them will appear out of the building. I realise I haven't thought about what I'm going to say but perhaps that's because you shouldn't have to rehearse what you're going to say to your own mother.

There isn't a gate or a proper path to the barn door, so I stop a few feet away. I'm feeling quite sick, and I take the wilting sweet peas from my basket to grasp as an offering in my hands. They look as pathetic as I feel.

Closing my eyes I take the first step, then manage another, then more until I finally reach the entranceway. I search for where to knock.

But I don't need to knock in the end because I see her. She looks up from where she's sitting at the rickety table as though she feels my presence, then she starts blinking madly at me.

"Pip?" she says, my name as a question. She doesn't believe that I'm really here. I can't believe that I *am* really here.

Any hope of her looking better is now forgotten. She looks worse, far worse, as pitiful as the flowers in my sweating palm. Dropping them to the floor I almost run to her as she tries to get up from the table.

"Sit down, mam," I say quietly, "there's no need to get up on my account."

I force a smile because all I care about is making her feel better in any small way I can. When she smiles back, the macabre sight frightens me, but I try not to avert my eyes. I would still hate to upset her whatever she may have done.

"Pip, my Pip," she says over and over as I kiss her cheek and hold her fragile hands as tightly as I dare. It's as though they might shatter.

I sit in the only other chair at the small table, and we stare at each other for long enough. I'm terrified now her heart might fail from the shock, and it would be all my fault. Her eyes stray around my face, drinking in the sight of me. My eyes stay fixed upon hers, so I don't have to look at what she's become.

The barn smells of summer damp, the foulness sitting in my nostrils so I could gip. How can she stand it here and where is 'he'?

I won't be able to settle until I know we won't be disturbed. There are so many questions I want to ask but I'm on edge, thinking "he" will make an appearance at any moment. I must try harder to gather my thoughts and make the best of what time we have.

"I've missed you," she says in almost a whisper, tears sparkling her eyes.

It's on the tip of my tongue to say the same, but I stop myself because it will upset her to hear it. Instead, I ask, "Have you eaten today?" It's all I can think of to say.

She nods her head even though I suspect it's a lie.

"I hoped you'd come here. Some days I'd wake up and think today's the day our Pip will appear and … and now you have. You can only imagine how happy I am."

"I think I understand," I say, "I hoped I'd find you in better health."

She runs her thumbs over the back of my hands. It doesn't really soothe me though as it would have done once.

"You're all the tonic I need and I'm sure I can recover now," she says, "will you have a pot of tea?"

"I don't have time, mam, I wish I did. Da has gone out delivering furniture and he'll worry about me when he gets back. I came on a whim." I pause and look around, "Is he here?"

She's staring at our hands.

"No, love he's … he's working. He'll be glad for me that you came to visit."

Somehow, I don't believe a word of it though I'd like to.

"Is he good to you?" I ask, the question sounding too pointed. I haven't time to faff about.

She still doesn't look up so I can't see what's going on behind her eyes.

69

"Oh yes, he is, don't worry about that. But Pip, I've missed you all so bad. I knew I was caught between the devil and the deep blue sea, but it's been crippling."

I grasp the moment like a starving woman.

"Come home!" I say loudly, "Da's feelings for you never changed and Liam will forgive you in time. Just come home, mam, get your shawl and come back with me. We can wait halfway at the beck, and I'll get da. He'll carry you home if needs be, you see if he doesn't."

My voice is growing frantic, I'm sure my expression will be the same. She pulls her hands away and gets up from the table. For a moment I get a glimpse of my old my mother getting up to make a pot of tea like the old days at *Sunnyside*.

"If I could, I would. I can't come back with you, but if you call here every week, I'll start to feel better. I feel better already."

She puts the kettle on the coals, then walks to the dresser for the tea. Two raggedy chairs that don't match sit by the fire and I picture her sitting there with that man on an evening. What do they talk about; do they discuss us or avoid the subject of us like the plague? Both scenarios sadden me.

The unmade bed at the far side of the room looks as though she's just climbed out of it. My mother of old would never have left a bed unmade, not for all the tea in China.

"Da said you fell in love," I say, the words struggling to come out of my mouth.

She keeps her back to me. "Did he?"

"Did you fall in love, mam?"

I can't let it go. I need to hear her say it, so I can believe it.

"Love comes in many forms," she says.

I have my answer. She's using one of her many sayings to distract me, I know it now. This is what she always did when she wanted to avoid a subject, the time is ticking away and she's wasting it. Perhaps I'm expecting too much too soon, perhaps the next time I come she'll be ready to tell me.

My father and Liam will be on their way back by now. Sitting here talking in circles won't get us anywhere and a panic rises at the thought of them coming to find me. I want to get home. The chair scrapes across the flags as I scrabble quickly to my feet, suddenly finding it difficult to breathe in the dampness. She looks up from pouring the milk startled at the sound.

"Mam, I'm sorry, I'll have to get going. I'll come back again but right now I need to get home."

I remember the flowers and head to the open door to pick them up from the floor as they lay scattered in the entrance where I left them. They need to sit in water, so they can revive and give this dreadful room some life.

Two flowers sit in my hand when the sun suddenly disappears and a shadow appears on the ground, swamping me in darkness. I have a creeping sensation at the back of my neck before I even look up. When I do I see the broad silhouette of man and I shudder.

I can't see his expression as his features are in shadow, but I know this man instantly just from his build and his scent.

My mind jumps to that day when I was losing consciousness in the snowstorm and the stranger who slung me over his shoulder.

Putting my hand over my eyes now so I can see better, his expression somehow makes me feel like a lamb to the slaughter again. I glance quickly over my shoulder into the semi-gloom of the barn to see my mother's ashen face staring our way.

Oh, mam please come home, I think, closing my eyes to the look of horror on her face.

Just come home with me, let us flee far away from this terrible world you have chosen to live in while we still can.

Chapter 11
1892 - Jarvis

Pip looks every bit the elegant young lady offering tea to her guest except for her shaking hands and a slight mottled rash on her neck. Her nerves are obvious but then her mother has just been murdered, and the police are sniffing around asking questions. I would think it only fitting under the circumstances.

"Will you have a biscuit?" she asks, nudging a plate of oatcakes in my direction.

Taking one from the plate I munch away but nobody joins me.

"Lovely," I say, rubbing my hands together to be rid of the crumbs, "I'm famished after that long walk. I suppose you're both used to it."

Charlie looks my way, no sign of nerves unlike his daughter.

"Ay, but to be fair I use my horse and cart more nowadays," he says, "I'm no spring chicken anymore."

I smile at him, and glance at Pip who isn't with us. She has a faraway look in her eye as she blows her tea and sips it. She's always been a bit of a mystery, always far from the feral creature you would expect living out in the wild. Her mother was the same; how she carried herself was the same, yet everybody likes to make out she was as common as muck. Ma's right, there are plenty of people who won't bother shedding a tear over the loss of Orla Metcalfe and that's putting it politely.

Pip notices me watching her and quickly tries to mirror my expression, her cheeks flushing but she fails to convince me. I'd love to know what she's thinking.

I ponder how to begin. After what she did to them will my condolences be welcome? It might actually draw a reaction from Charlie, and I have a sense Pip will appreciate the gesture.

"My condolences, Mr Metcalfe, Miss Metcalfe," I say stiffly.

Pip offers a weak smile of acknowledgement. Charlie says nothing.

I pause, assessing their reaction.

"Well, I've no doubt you'll both have plenty to be getting on with, and I better make tracks before too long with this snow. I'm sure you know why I'm here; I only need to ask a few questions and I'll be on my way," I say.

That's not strictly true. If I'm not satisfied with the answers to the questions, they'll have to accompany me back to the station. But there's no need for me to jump the gun and make them both twitchy.

They exchange brief glances, but I can't read anything from that alone. It's far too early to draw any conclusions and nervous people act out of character, so it's in everyone's best interest to be laid back in my approach to questioning.

"Does my daughter need to be here?" Charlie asks.

Pip suddenly becomes alert, sitting up in her chair.

"That's alright, da, I'd rather be here. I've no doubt the inspector will want to ask me some questions eventually, so I'd rather get it over with."

My eyes fix to her face as she speaks. It's surrounded by a cloud of blonde hair which is almost white, the likes of which I've never seen before except on young children. She's so quietly spoken I must strain to hear her words.

Charlie turns back to me and nods his tacit permission to continue, and I'm suddenly uncomfortable under their gaze. My assuredness is faltering, and I'm almost self-conscious with an odd feeling of being aware of every muscle in my body all at once. I clear my throat and fold my arms on the table to steady myself.

"So, I imagine the first question won't come as a surprise: where were you both on the night of … of Mrs Metcalfe's …" I hesitate to use the obvious word and finish the sentence, "on the night of the 12th?"

Charlie's right, Pip shouldn't be here. This is her mother we're talking about and it's all so recent, it must still be like a gaping wound. She takes a sip of tea, but her gulp is too loud.

"Miss Metcalfe, I really think it might be better if I spoke to your father alone. This situation will be distressing for you to say the least and there's no reason to put yourself through it at present."

She shakes her head dismissively saying, "I'll still be upset in an hour, a day, a week, so you will just have to forgive me if I lose my composure at any point."

Her bottom lip is trembling slightly. I'm not sure whether to continue but then I look out of the window at the thickening snow and decide to push ahead.

"Of course, if you insist. So, where were you, Mr Metcalfe?"

"I was here, as was Pip. We can vouch for each other, but I've no idea if that would stand up in court."

I hold his steady gaze for so long his face becomes a blur. When I look at Pip her head is bowed which only adds to the awkwardness of the situation.

"It will be useful for a jury to know this, yes, but of course, you are members of the same family," I say, wondering why he's worried about what a court would deduce, if indeed he is telling the truth.

Charlie shrugs but doesn't look irritable or agitated. That open and honest face of his will stand him in good stead, but I've been in this game long enough not to be hoodwinked by that. Once a fourteen-year-old boy swore blind he hadn't stolen and sold a horse. He sat there like butter wouldn't melt in his mouth all wide-eyed and sincere and he had the lot of us convinced. He even had us feeling bad for him. After a bit more digging it turned out his parents were in the dark the same as us that he'd stolen five horses from various villages over the course of two years.

"I understand," is all Charlie says.

I've no idea how to substantiate his statement. They live such a remote life, it's unlikely they crossed paths with anyone else that week, let alone that day.

I wish I'd taken my coat off, the room is far too hot. If I take it off now though it will look like I'm losing my nerve. I need to tread carefully.

"Your daughter's testimony may not be sufficient an alibi, Mr Metcalfe, and I'm afraid in many people's eyes you have ample reason." I glance between them to try and increase the pressure but it's no use they won't budge. "Well, let's leave that for now, there is something else I need to discuss with you."

Pip shuffles uncomfortably in her seat whereas Charlie sits perfectly still, barely raising an eyebrow though his jaw tightens slightly. Perhaps my tactic is paying off. I feel a flicker of self-satisfaction in my gut.

"There was an item found at the scene which we now have at the police station."

I pause again, searching Charlie's face for a glimmer of recognition or surprise. His brow furrows slightly as Pip looks at him. He doesn't turn his head.

"And what might that be?" he asks with a small chuckle.

He's no fool, old Charlie, he knows when he's being played. But playing people is all part of the job. I move this piece; they move that one—it bides us time and helps us to analyse people and situations.

Pip's eyes are almost filling her face like a deer. She looks terrified, trapped and it unsettles me briefly. She shakes her head though I never asked her a question.

"A yellow pencil was found at the scene," I say, "a yellow *carpenter's* pencil from Brierley's in Wakefield. Apparently, the distinctive colour is to make them easily found amongst other tools. But you'll know more about that than me Mr Metcalfe, I'm sure."

As startled as each other, Charlie and I both whip our heads towards Pip as a strangled laugh escapes her.

It's all out there now and there's no hiding my intentions, no more pussy footing around the edges.

"Inspector Blackburn, do you think my father would be daft enough to murder my mother and then leave a pencil at the scene that points the finger of suspicion squarely at him?"

My attention returns to her father. I don't know if he would be daft enough, I barely know the man. This is a desperate girl on the cusp of losing everything. She's lost her mother and now she might be at risk of losing her father. She will believe what she needs to believe.

"That's what I'm here to find out, Miss Metcalfe," I say, "but if we can't find a plausible answer, you will both need to accompany me to the station for a more formal interview."

Her face falls at my terse response. The small fire has gone from her belly, and she looks close to tears. She gave me fair warning she might lose her composure, but now I have a flood of empathy making my eyes drop to the table.

She pats her father's hand then gets up to go to the window of the kitchen area. Each of the four panes of glass have steamed from the heat inside and she wipes one of the panes with the palm of her hand. Her shoulders are straight, and her blonde hair hangs to the middle of her back.

"Well, I don't think we'll be going anywhere for the time being, I'm afraid, inspector," she says, still staring through the window.

Striding across the room to join her I'm now horrified to see a featureless sky that blurs my sight, nothing but whiteness. I rush to open the door to see snow drifting halfway up the entrance to the cottage.

I turn to look at my hosts who look neither mocking nor sympathetic to the predicament I brought on myself.

Closing the door, a cold hand grips my stomach and I have the strangest feeling.

Why didn't they tell me; did they know this would happen? I can't help but wonder now if these two so-called innocents have just played me at my own game.

Chapter 12
Maureen - 1884

"I just can't put my finger on it, but that Pip Metcalfe gives me the creeps," Ivy says, fluffing her curls in the mirror over the mantle. I take great pains with those curls, making sure they are exactly the same size and shape.

She's only young but she takes a pride in her appearance I think smiling at my daughter's reflection. I take pride too, as my mother did before me, for all the good it does me. It's wasted on my Walter that's for sure, I could walk around in my birthday suit, heaven forbid, and he'd carry on reading the paper.

"Why's that do you think then?" I ask her as she flounces to sit down on the settee. Her dress for school is still better than every other girl's Sunday best. I'm handy with a needle and thread though I say so myself, often sewing late into the night after I've finished in the shop.

"Oh, I don't know, it's the way she looks at me, more than anything. It's like she knows something I don't and she's enjoying herself."

I drain my teacup and mull over Ivy's comment about Pip. I don't feel the same way about her, if anything she seems almost shy around me which is quite sweet.

Ivy and I usually don't have long in between customers, but I can't afford to shut the shop for my dinner and breaks. We're often interrupted.

"Ivy, my love, you'll come to know in this life that people will always be jealous of you. You're beautiful with devoted parents who aren't doing too badly for themselves. We see to it that we give you the best we can afford, and so other people think you're full of yourself, with ideas above your station. But as my old dad used to say, "What others think of you is none of your business.""

Is she listening to me, or has she moved on to thinking about something else? I hope not as I consider a mother's most important role is to pass on nuggets of wisdom, especially to their daughters. I'm glad we had a girl as sons only seem to hang around until their head gets turned by a pretty face. Then their mothers seem to be out of favour and cast adrift.

Thinking about it, I suppose Jarvis is the exception. He's very good to his mother and she always speaks highly of him. So proud she is, but not in a bragging way. If I had a son, I'd like one like Jarvis Blackburn.

"Have you seen her hair?" Ivy says, "What with pale hair, pale skin, blue eyes it's like she's almost transparent, invisible even. Then she can watch on unnoticed. She's odd if you ask me."

I conjure up a picture of Pip Metcalfe in my mind. To me she's very pretty, very polite and … docile, that's the word. She's no bother, not like that mother of hers. Now Orla Metcalfe is trouble walking around on two legs.

"She's had a harder life than you, Ivy. Living out in the sticks with nobody but her family around for company isn't good for a child, it's not healthy. She trails around with her mother like a puppy dog and hangs onto her every word just the same. It's odd you're right but I think Pip's harmless enough."

I still don't think I've made my point.

"We're fortunate," I say, "we have a lot more than most people around here. Mind, we work for it."

Ivy heaves a sigh and stares into the fire. She could be on a poster, she's so bonny, I think. She's the reason I work as hard as I do, because Walter spends so much down the pub and my daughter isn't cut out for hard graft. I see her as a beautiful but delicate rose, that needs sheltering from harsh weather. Perhaps one day Jarvis will shelter her as well as I do if I can do a bit of matchmaking in a year or two before he's snapped up.

The shop doorbell goes, and I touch Ivy's shoulder as I go past. She picks up her latest book to read. *Heidi* it's called; I've no idea what it's about because I don't read but she's getting through it quick enough so she must be enjoying it.

I stop in my tracks briefly when I see who is waiting for me. Spooky to think we were only just this minute talking about them. Now, *Orla* Metcalfe definitely gives me the creeps.

"Afternoon, Mrs Metcalfe, Pip," I say, fixing a smile.

Orla returns my greeting while the girl stands holding her mother's hand. She gives me a warm smile and I just can't help my own smile widening in return.

She's quite endearing I realise now Ivy's brought her to my attention.

"You're in a bit later today," I say, straightening the boxes of baccy at the side of the counter though they're straight enough already.

"Yes, I had to wait for Charlie to finish a delivery," Orla says without looking up from the potatoes she's busy feeling, "I don't need much today though. Just five pounds of these and half a pound of sugar will do."

That's strange, she normally comes in and buys the shop up or at least buys as much as she can afford in one go. Well, mine is not to reason why, I think bagging up her goods as per instructions. I pass them over one by one then she offers her money before turning to the child.

"Go sit with your da a minute, Pip, I'll be out in a minute."

Pip smiles at me, then says goodbye. I give her a half-smile, but I can't speak because something's off, I know it. Her mother wants to talk to me on her own, something has got to be off.

"You might want to put the closed sign up a minute, Mrs Davies," she says calmly after Pip is well out of earshot.

I stare straight through her before traipsing over to the door. Sliding the bolt, I'm suddenly afraid; I can't work out if I'm afraid of Orla Metcalfe herself, or what she's going to tell me.

"Is Ivy in the back?" she asks.

I nod.

"You might want to shut the door a minute then."

I don't even question it I just do as she asks like I'm sleep-walking.

Standing at the back of the counter, it's as if my feet are sinking into the floorboards. I hold onto the rail where I hang my paper bags to steady myself. I do it discreetly because I don't want her to have the satisfaction of knowing she's rattling me.

"I'm sorry, Mrs Davies, Maureen, I've come to tell you something I think it's only right you should know."

My mind goes quickly to the conversation I've just had with our Ivy, and I have a wave of nausea. Are these two a pair of witches and that's why they manage to unsettle the whole village?

Get a hold of yourself, Maureen, I think, you're becoming hysterical now.

"Oh, what's that then?" I ask finally.

Her face is pinched like she's worried sick about something.

"It's your Walter," she says, "I'm sorry to be the one to tell you but he's … he's been seeing Nora Granger from the *Rose & Crown* and I thought it was only right you should know. I don't like the thought of people talking behind your back."

I blink at her a few times as I take in what she's just said. My Walter, having the gumption to see somebody else behind my back. She's off her rocker more than I thought this one. I let out a laugh that rings around the shop like an echo.

"You're having me on," I say, my smile so tight it's hurting my face.

"He's been seeing her quite a while from what I gather. Charlie says he's seen them in other villages; he's only just let the cat out of the bag, or I would have told you afore. It's just not right."

It's a good job the counter is between us, or I'd slap her face. I've never done anything remotely like that before, but I could do it now.

"How dare you?" I say quietly, so her green eyes open wide, "As if you dare to come in here and tell me such a thing. My Walter loves me, he loves our Ivy, he'd never lower himself to have it away with a flighty type like Nora Granger. You've come to stir up trouble, I know. You just want the heat to be taken off you and your wily set up on the moors."

She looks at me like I've slapped her face anyway. I'm not sure what I mean by wily other than her appearing from nowhere one day and her daughter is never in school. People talk around here; people talk a lot and sometimes facts get misconstrued. I bet that's what happened here with this silly story she has the cheek to stand here and tell me.

"Mrs Davies, I can assure you I didn't want to come here today. If you don't believe me or choose to ignore me then there's nothing that I can do about it. I'll leave you to your day, my job is done here. I thought you should know and now you do."

She picks her basket up from the floor while I think of something to heckle after her. I fancy a nice parting shot, but I can't think of anything. I can't think of anything except Walter kissing Norma Granger, holding Norma Granger … and far, far worse.

She slides the bolt and heads off to her family without a care in the world while she's just tipped mine upside down and stamped on it.

I run over to the door and bolt it shut again, my chest heaving as I slump to the floor, gasping for breath. I know how long it is that I sit with my back against the door after Orla Metcalfe leaves: it's over half an hour. I hear the doorknob rattle umpteen times and even a couple of knocks, but I ignore them because they can't see me behind all the adverts for this and that pasted on the glass door. I eventually hear a huddle of women outside chuntering about why we might be closed when I never shut up shop before six o'clock.

I know exactly how long I'm in that state because I eventually go into the back room to see Ivy who's in the same place where I left her, head bowed engrossed in her book. I check the clock and it says twenty-five to five. Walter will be home at ten past five for his tea and a bath before he goes out. There's a roll in my stomach when I think about him, then Norma. Is this a vicious rumour or is it true that there's never any smoke without fire? Am I being naive?

Orla Metcalfe is no fool and you wouldn't put yourself through the ordeal she's just had for nothing.

I perch on the other end of the settee and sit a moment until Ivy glances my way.

"Hadn't you better get tea on?" she says.

I'm sure I look as white as a sheet, but she doesn't notice.

Fury sits in my chest, so I must close my eyes and swallow it down hard. God only knows what I'll do to Walter when he gets in. I get up and walk the few steps to the tiny kitchen to peel some carrots and potatoes that will go nicely with the pork chops I've had in the range since late morning.

But I don't do anything to Walter when he eventually arrives home. I only fill up his bath and serve him his tea as normal. Then he wanders off to the pub just before seven to fall in with the doors while I cut out a pattern for a new dress for Ivy. As I listen to the shears slicing through the crisp cotton, my favourite sound, I finally manage to stop my heart from hammering in my chest.

In the half an hour before Walter returns, I've done a lifetime of thinking. There's our Ivy in the middle of all this. She's more important than him and me and the way I see it, I must put my daughter first. That's what any good mother would do. Ivy needs two parents who can love and provide for her in this house and one of them leaving just isn't a risk I'm prepared to take.

So, when I find out eventually from Mrs Wilkes that Orla Metcalfe has left her family to go live with some other bloke and only a few miles away, well it's difficult to put into words exactly how I feel about that woman.

Chapter 13
Pip - 1892

I take down the clothes from the airer over the fire and start folding socks. One pair look and feel unfamiliar, far softer wool than the others.

"Here, I'll take those," Jarvis says, taking them gently from my hands. I don't expect you to sort my washing out."

His face is flushed when he says almost shyly, "I'm thankful you have a brother—I'd much rather be wearing his under-things than your father's, I can tell you." A small laugh tries to hide his embarrassment.

I smile unable to meet his eyes, deciding to change the subject to ease our mutual discomfort.

"We never know how long we're likely to be cut-off by the weather," I say, "we need to make sure we're always prepared for it by the end of the summer."

I think it's possibly better not to mention the twenty-one days we were stranded that time. Who knows, it could thaw enough tomorrow so he can get back to the village, so he'll be worrying unnecessarily. It's not a pleasant thought for myself either. My father can escape to the workshop while I'm stuck in here with a police inspector watching my every move and analysing my every word.

At first, Jarvis thought we were just being overdramatic when we told him he'd have to stay the night.

"Surely not," he said, "my mother will be worried and there's far too much to be done at the station."

"I'm sure your mother will work it out, inspector and as for your work, it will still be there when you get back," my father told him. "Sometimes the weather takes the decisions out of our hands, and in my experience it's better all round if you just accept it."

I think Jarvis had the idea the snow would go as quickly as it came and just disappear like magic before bedtime. If he went to the window once, he went a thousand times to look out and check. My father and I were too distracted to notice the snow drifting higher; we should have kept an eye on the weather situation. Then again, it's not often you have the police at your house asking questions about …

I sit down in the fireside chair to finish my folding, keeping my head low. It's still like a body blow when I remember that my mother's not with us anymore. While ever she was alive, I always lived in hope of her return. Hope is the most precious of gifts I've found out now.

"I really thought I could make it back," Jarvis says, "life is hard out here, I don't know how you manage, Miss Metcalfe, I really don't."

Placing the pile of clean washing in the basket I flop back in my chair to give him my attention.

"I wish you'd call me Pip, at least while you're staying under our roof. It just seems silly to be so formal."

He shakes his head and runs a hand through his hair. He looks so much younger out of his suit with his sleeves rolled up and collar undone. I've never really looked at him before. Jarvis became the policeman in the village to me, like he's not a man in his own right, not even a person.

"We might have found ourselves in extraordinary informal circumstances, but my reason for being here still couldn't be more formal. Nothing has changed," he says.

I feel like I've had a ticking off, like when my father told me off for saying Liam was being a right pain in the arse. He was mind, and saying backside wasn't anywhere near satisfying enough for once, it just didn't relieve my frustration. Little brothers can be beyond trying.

"I see," I say, when I don't, "well, to address your concerns, we don't really notice the weather out here much to be honest, snow is usually just a mild inconvenience. We always keep a huge stack of dried food in my father's workshop, so we never run short."

He sits at the table watching me as though I'm a case study in a laboratory. He will be keen not to miss anything he could potentially use against me at a later date.

"Don't you ever get a dose of cabin fever?" he asks, "I think I might."

He's looking out of the window. It won't help his case as there's nothing to see but snow for endless miles like a white sea.

"Don't you ever feel like you're acting out your life on the stage with all those people watching your every move?"

The corners of his mouth twitch and he looks over at me, his eyes full of humour.

"Is that how you would feel?"

I get up to fill the kettle from the bucket of melted snow he kindly fetched this morning. It gave him something to do for all of two minutes.

"Yes, I'm afraid it is. Perhaps it's because I haven't known any other way of life, but I always have an eyrie sensation of being watched when I go into Ackley."

"That's because you are being watched, you're quite right. I've never thought about it like that before. We all know each other's business and we all sit in judgement of it. It's funny how we live only a few miles apart, yet we lead such different lives."

Bimble strolls over and lies on her back by his feet. He reaches down to stroke her but then she gets on her way, independent, the mistress of her own destiny.

"That's another thing," he says, "I've never even thought about having a pet never mind had one. Ma would have said it was just another mouth to feed."

"Bimble's not a pet though I love her, she earns her keep by keeping the vermin down."

He chuckles suddenly and I pop my head around the dresser door to look at him.

"I just had a thought about what Ivy Davies would do if a cat dropped a mouse at her feet. I'd like to be a fly on the wall to see that, by that I would."

He sounds and looks like Liam would, like a cheeky young boy not a fine, upstanding keeper of the peace. I shake my head and smile as he picks up the spoon in the bowl of sugar in the middle of the table and starts fiddling with it. There's a bored man if ever there was one.

"Do you read?" I ask.

He looks startled by the turn in the conversation. "Read?"

"Yes, read, you know, books. Works of fiction, poetry."

He stops faffing with the sugar for a minute, spoon mid-air to give the question some thought.

"I read *The Adventures of Huckleberry Finn* a few years ago. I'm lying, I read two chapters but never got around to finishing it. I've mainly been reading textbooks since I can remember. Why do you ask?"

His head cocks to one side, no doubt poised to hear an interesting response from me. I march over to the table to stand next to him and he leans away from me in his chair slightly. He looks worried now, wrongfooted for once wondering what I'm about to do.

"Well, if you're not going to get under my feet for however long you're here, we need to think of something quickly to keep you occupied," I say, putting the lid back on the sugar bowl with a clatter.

From the corner of my eye, my father comes in from the workshop and I watch him take a step backwards at the sound of our laughter.

Chapter 14
1889 - Liam

Does he know who I am? He must do yet he's not looking the side I'm on.

He's acting as though there's only him in the taproom when it's crammed with people laughing and talking while he sits there alone, eyes glazed with too much beer.

I usually drink in the *Rose & Crown* with my mates, but tonight I caved and came here instead. I've come to see the man who stole my mother, the man who ripped our family apart. This is how I think of him when I lay awake in the middle of the night.

My mother leaving was like taking a bullet, but to up sticks and live barely four miles away from us has served to rub salt in the wound so it's stinging like hell.

Foster was a faceless man until tonight and I'm not sure yet whether I feel better or worse for seeing him. It's helped my curiosity yet fuelled the fire in the pit of my stomach that I've come to live with.

He's a lot younger than my father and not bad looking I suppose in a battered and worn sort of way. But handsome is as handsome does as my mother said once to bring me down a peg or two when she heard me bragging to Pip about a girl at school calling me it. My mother wouldn't be taken in by a handsome face. Even if she could have left my father for such a stupid reason, she could never have left us.

Bradley Foster. I wish I'd never found out his name because now it scoots around my mind all day long, even when I'm busy. Twice he's looked in my direction, once when he was stood but two men away at the bar. Both times he's looked through me. The barman knows what he drinks, so he doesn't even need to speak to him. Braithwaite's dark is his chosen drink so that's another discovery to add to the list. I'm building up quite a picture, but it's a picture I'd rather stamp into the earth with the toe of my boot like a ciggie stub.

I know Pip's been to see my mother. She had a guilty look about her that day she was out when we got back, and I knew straight away where she'd been. I couldn't help hating her for weeks afterwards for betraying us and it took all the strength I had to be civil towards her. I'd have had it out with her, but I didn't want to upset da. Now, I know it's not worth it because Pip has always been like my second mother, so what would be the point in losing two mothers? I'd only be shooting myself in the foot, nobody else.

I have a sudden realisation as I watch Foster swig his ale and it's one that surprises me that I've only just thought of it: at this very minute my mother is sitting alone in that place where they shacked up together, that place my father told us about that's in the grounds of Kettlethorpe Farm.

Before I know it, I'm picturing my mother there and wondering what she'll be doing. I shouldn't want to know or even care what she's doing, that was the pact I made with myself when she left.

Foster's head turns slowly in my direction. I catch his eye for less than a second before I look away and down the last of my pint in one, slapping it on the bar. I'm off home.

I can't resist one last look over after I nod at old Bert the landlord and turn on my heel to leave. Foster is still watching me, but I don't know this time if he's looking straight through me because I don't hang around long enough to find out.

The sudden chill of the early evening makes me pull my collar up and push my hands in my pockets. I'm shocked now by my mother's face popping into my head yet again and I shake my head to try and be rid of it. She's got such a lovely face, or she did until he came along and made her so lovesick so she could barely eat. If that's what love does to you, then they can keep it, thanks all the same.

I can't help thinking every time I walk back to *Sunnyside* about how life should be if things were different. I should by rights be going home to see my mother and father and our Pip now. I should be kicking off my boots and telling them that Ken Morton, Sarah's da had told me earlier that Sarah's soft on me. I thought he was having me on at first or it was the drink talking. If I think about it, I like her too, the little I've seen of her since we left school. She's got shiny brown hair and nice white teeth when she smiles. She's pretty but quiet, a bit like our Pip in that way.

Instead, I'll just get in and have a quick brew before I go up to bed out of the way. I'm in a mood, I can't help it and Pip sometimes gets the brunt of my moods. I apologise afterwards if I've been a bit snappy with her, and she says she understands, and I think she does. Perhaps that's why I do it, but it's not right when all she thinks about is our da and me.

I don't normally notice the old wooden signpost to Kettlethorpe but tonight I stare up at it. It's just before the turn off to home. I study the signpost for a minute like I'm wondering where it came from. If I don't try and figure things out with my mother, Pip will always be getting the worst of me when she should be getting the best.

She doesn't deserve it and I've just realised tonight there's only me who can sort it out.

Taking in a deep breath of cold air I hold it at the back of my throat. It feels like the biggest step, I will have made in my life so far.

I let out my fear in one huge, long puff, watching the cloud of moisture disappear down towards the dark track home without me. I can follow it still, but instead I turn left and stand still, hands still firmly in pockets.

You must go tonight, Liam lad, I think. Tomorrow you will lose momentum and then be back to your old self, seething with bitterness at all that we've lost.

So, I carry on out of the deserted village. This road ahead is not well travelled, and never before by me, so I'll have to watch my step in the blackness. It's the wrong time of day to be going anywhere but home. Foster will know this road like the back of his hand, traipsing up and down it every night. Thinking of him takes my mind to my mother like always.

I know our life was odd to most people, but we couldn't have been happier. My father is a good listener, and he always had a look on his face when my mother was talking, like a little half-smile, and his eyes were what I would call warm. I'd heard my mother read enough romantic poems by then to know what that look meant. We were just happy.

Then Pip and me would go up for a good night's sleep before doing it all again. We used to whisper through the curtain before we went to sleep about going to Ireland one day when we were grown-ups. There was so much to look forward to and my mother brought her home to life for us. The sea, the landscape, the people especially, we wanted to meet them all.

I remember my mother telling us she had seven brothers and sisters in all, and they grew up in a house not much bigger than ours. They were never at home much as her father was always looking for an excuse to pick a fight when he was around. Many left Ireland she said because they were poor or starving, but my mother's family had enough money and plenty to eat. Fancy someone having to leave so many people they loved behind, including their own mother, just to get away from one nasty person. She must have been desperate when she ran away on her own to live here at such a young age. I can't imagine travelling alone on a boat even now and I'm not a young girl. I always thought she was brave.

If she hadn't met my father, who knows what could have become of her. My blood boils now like it often does when I think about the villagers—surely, they could have made her more welcome instead of shunning her for years.

I'm shocked when something wet trickles into my mouth. I'm crying; for god's sake I'm bloody crying. Wiping my cheeks with my coat sleeve I think about the white hanky my mother always made me carry. I had four and I put them on the fire when she left. Pip caught me, and it's a good job because I was going to burn her books and that would have been sacrilegious, Pip told me. I didn't know what it meant, so I looked it up afterwards and it's about the most wicked thing a person could do.

Pip had me in a tight hold when she said it so I couldn't run away like I wanted. In the end, I just stood like that with her for ages until I went up to bed feeling a bit calmer but embarrassed by then.

I'm glad I didn't burn those books now because the only people it would have hurt would have been my father and me, but worst of all … our Pip.

Chapter 15
1892 - Jarvis

She rarely sits down all day. I've noticed over the last two days that Pip Metcalfe is in perpetual motion until she settles down of an evening after tea. If she's not washing clothes, or feeding the cat or the horse, she's sweeping or cleaning or changing beds or cooking. This cottage is like a new pin as ma would say and Pip does it all, if not exactly cheerfully, then contentedly. I've been watching her a lot since I've been snowed in here, and now I don't think it's because there's not much else to do.

I drop my head back and sigh. I'm past bored and I've got to get out of here, but where can I go? Pip's upstairs so I wander to the door to get some air. At least the snow has stopped even if it's too cold for it to thaw yet. I glance down the path we've shovelled to Charlie Metcalfe's workshop and the fork to the stable next door. I see the smoke puffing from his workshop chimney and sigh again, leaning against the threshold. I think it's high time Charlie and I had another chat.

Taking my coat and the scarf ma knit me from the hook, I pull on my boots. They're not really adequate but it's only a short walk to the workshop so I'm sure I'll live.

It feels good to be outside after so long. I take in the snowy landscape thinking I could have stepped into another world. It's like I've been living in another world too; the inhabitants here are different to any I've known before. Looping my scarf around my neck again for extra warmth I think I've finally worked out why it is they seem so different.

I suppose Charlie and Pip are straightforward folk, that's the most apt description I've been able to think of. There's a charm about them I've never noticed with anyone in Ackley. They don't appear to want anything other than what they've got already. Even ma is always getting a new dress or making a new cushion when we must have ten on rotation each season already. And Ivy, she must have twenty dresses, her ma sees to that. In fact, I don't recall seeing her in the same dress twice, except that green one if I think about it. I'll have to earn a pot of money if I'm to stand a chance at keeping up with her lifestyle.

I stop in my tracks realising that every time I think of Ivy it's not in a fond way. It was the same before I came here, but now I've had time to notice it.

Bella snorts in the stable and I nip inside to see her. She's snug enough in here and well fed and watered by the look of her. Stroking the white of her dappled neck she turns to push her nose into my hand. She's a beauty and a lovely nature I can sense it. I've noticed Pip disappearing with an apple down here a time or two in between feeding times every day to enjoy her company. I should have done the same myself.

I can't stall for time any longer. Stepping outside I knock on the door of Charlie's workshop and wait. He appears after a few seconds in his overalls, looking at me blankly like he's never met me before in his life.

"I thought I'd have a change of scenery," I say quickly, "that's if you don't mind, of course."

He pulls the door back, saying, "Not at all, step inside, inspector. But I might have to put you to work if *you* don't mind."

We smile at each other before I glance at the piece he's making. I look again but longer this time. Piece doesn't do it justice, it's more a work of art; the barley twist wood turning of the dresser top is just beautiful.

"I'll have to be a labourer," I tell him running my hand over the carving, "I'd hate to ruin all your hard work."

The workshop is immaculate, there's a place for everything and everything in its place. *Metcalfe & Son* are the only furniture makers for miles, and I recall ma once said Charlie will let you buy from him on tick, so you don't have to shell out the whole amount in one go.

"Do you mind if I carry on?" he says now, "Time is money when you work for yourself."

The smell of cut wood mixed with coal and linseed oil is powerful and not unpleasant. I picture him and Liam working together day after day in here and wonder if they get on each other's nerves.

Picking up a small chisel he resumes whittling the pattern on the left-hand drawer. I watch over his shoulder a minute until he says without looking up, "There's a chair over there that could do with a bit of an oil if you want to make yourself useful. Finishing off is normally one of our Liam's jobs."

That will do me nicely I think, you can't really mess up a job like oiling wood. I grab the stained cotton cloth to make a start and we work silently for a few minutes.

"Nay lad, not up and down, run in circles, working your way out to the edge; you'll get a more even coating that way."

Bloody hell, I can't even get a simple task right, I think. I do as I'm told but quickly think how to change the subject. I don't want to bombard him with questions, or he'll feel ambushed. I need to make sure I'm more subtle about it.

"Pip runs a tight ship in the house," I say eventually, dipping my cloth in the bucket of oil again, "you could eat your dinner off the floor if you'd a mind to."

He nods with his back to me, saying, "Ay, she's a worker, but then we all are. There's always plenty for us to do out here."

Staring at his bent back I wonder what to say next to keep the conversation going.

"I bet she learnt a lot from her mother. How many years is it since she left now, five?"

Charlie spins round, chisel in hand, a disapproving look about him. Startled, I stop oiling the wood and stand up straight.

"Now, Inspector Blackburn if you don't mind, don't abuse our hospitality and use it as an extended period of questioning."

He's right of course, but then the elephant in the room is a bloody big one. He goes back to his work, and I buff the seat of the chair feeling like I've had a ticking off from my dad.

It's no good though, I'd be a fool to waste this opportunity just to spare his feelings.

"All I mean is, it can't have been easy for you all, but you seem to be coping well."

His shoulders slump further so his head drops forward as he sighs.

"Look, I know you're only doing your job and I don't hold it against you."

He turns and leans against the dresser, and I watch his agitated expression, wondering whether to go on or to just leave well alone. I know enough to keep quiet and wait for him to come to his own conclusion.

My heart races when he places the chisel on his workbench and rubs a hand at the back of his neck. I think he's made his decision.

"Right, as I've nothing to hide I might as well make it a bit easier for you," he says arms stretched either side of him on the dresser top, "yes, I had a wife who I loved, who I still love, as you'll no doubt be wondering, and I'll never recover properly from what happened but that's for me to worry about. As you know, in fact as all the village knows, my wife left me for another man. It won't be the first time its happened or the last. It'll not surprise you to hear we were devastated when she went but then we accepted it because that's what you have to do in life unless you're going to send yourself round the bend. Liam seemed on the surface to take it harder than Pip but even he got on with his life eventually. Now my wife has … gone," Charlie's voice cracks slightly, "but I had nothing to do with it and neither did my kids. Liam was at the pub with Sarah Morton's da, Ken all night and Pip was with me. That's it; that's all I can say about it and it's up to you to prove I'm lying if you can, but I'll be telling you the same thing to my dying breath."

His speech has upset me though I can't show it. Charlie said it in his usual matter-of-fact way, but there was no mistaking the pain hidden between each word he threw at me.

Picking up my cloth I go back to polishing my chair, slowly at first then really putting my back in it. I'd like to do a good job and then I'll see if there's anything else he needs doing. I might as well make myself useful while I'm here and I know Pip would be glad of it.

"Well then, we'll say no more about it whilst I'm staying under your roof," I tell him.

He stands quietly a moment and I feel his eyes on me as I work.

"That was too easy to my mind, lad. You're not saying you believe me, are you?" he asks.

I carry on with my task but throw a glance at him. If he's lying, he's the most convincing liar I've come across in all my years as a policeman. That yellow pencil is looking more like a red herring and less like a piece of evidence than it ever was. I heave a deep breath, my shoulders rising and falling with the effort.

"Ay, you're quite right, Mr Metcalfe," I say, "I believe you."

Standing back, I admire the gleaming patina of the polished wood with a sense of satisfaction then catch his eye.

A new feeling appears now as hold the level stare of Charlie Metcalfe: I have a sensation of utter contentment, possibly for the first time in my twenty-seven years.

For a while at least, and for however long it lasts, I've finally clocked off.

Chapter 16
1889 - Liam

It just seems ridiculous to knock on the door of my own mother's house. But then this is a ridiculous situation and she's not my mother any longer and this isn't even a house, just a barn.

From the small window above me, I can see there's a low candle burning. I don't know what she'll be doing on the other side of this door, but I'm intrigued to see how she spends her time. I lean my forehead against the wood of the barn door. I'm here now and I can try and deny it to myself, but I want to see her more than anything I've wanted before.

After two sharp raps, I stand back to wait. The flap of a startled owl flying away in the empty darkness startles me just the same.

The door opens but I can only see a shadowy figure. The shadow looks small and thin almost like a child.

"I never thought I'd see the day," she whispers.

I catch sight of her face and quickly look away when I notice the dress she's wearing. She used to fill it once but not anymore, it's now falling from her shoulders like a shapeless cloak.

She's ill; not worried, not lovesick, she's ill. I can tell from the rasp of her voice. Now we're face to face I really can't stomach going inside. Somehow, I feel safer out here. Once I go inside that house, I'll be trapped, she'll have me cornered like on the day she told me she was leaving.

The last time I saw her.

"Are you coming in, lad?"

I don't answer and I can't move even if I wanted to.

"Liam, you'll have to come in so I can shut out the weather. I don't expect you to care but I'm not feeling too good, and I need to get back to the fireside."

She's not too good, she said; I knew it. So, it looks like there's nothing else for it, I must step over the threshold, and listen to her close the door behind me like a prison guard slamming a cell door. My breath is picking up speed, the warmth of the room making my bones hurt because I'm so cold. Four miles in this weather is a very long way.

She shuffles across the room to sit in the chair by the dying fire, pulling an old blanket up to her chin. The blanket quivers like ripples in a river and I realise she's shivering.

I have no idea what to do. Should I stay standing or sit, but if I sit, where should I? More than anything I would like to ask her why she looks so terrible, but I can't seem to get the words to come out. When she stares across the room at me, she has a pathetic look in her eye which is disturbing me. To think, I wanted to waltz in here and give her a piece of my mind, give her short shrift as she would say. Now, I think it would be like shooting a lame horse; all the fight I built up with each step on the path here has suddenly gone out of me.

"I hope you aren't here looking for trouble, Liam," she says, "I'm not up to it in case you haven't noticed."

Her lips tilt slightly so she looks like a smiling skull. The sight disarms me—oh mam I think, it's as though you're not long for this world.

"What's up with you," I finally ask her. The words sound brittle like I don't care when suddenly I do.

"Just a chill, I think love. I'll be fine in a couple of days."

The image of Foster swigging ale in the pub makes me want to spit.

"So, he's left you like this to go out supping beer. I thought he was your knight in shining armour or whatever else he told you."

Her bloodshot eyes roll my way and make me slump down on a low buffet. I'm tired; I don't want to argue with a mother who's not fit to even stand. It's not a fair fight.

"Can I get you owt to eat?" I ask her.

A tear trickles down her cheek as she shakes her head, no doubt touched by the offer. It upsets me, makes me feel bad for being the person to put it there.

"No but thanks for offering. I've not got much appetite."

She can't be more than five stone wet through now, a stone less than when she was living with us. I remember her withering away before our eyes at home for long enough. I chose to ignore it then, but I think about it all the time now.

Every muscle in my body tenses and a realisation is dawning and threatening to break me.

This is the last time I will ever see my mother. I don't know why I can be so sure suddenly, but I am.

"I thought you'd run away to be happy," I say, dropping my head into my hands, "I hated you for it, but now I can't. You've taken that away from me along with everything else."

She sits in silence, and I can only hear the wind whistling. To think of her sitting in this place day after day, night after night—it's depressing. It doesn't make sense unless Foster didn't turn out to be all he promised. She can't have imagined this life surely.

"How could I ever be happy without my weans living with me?"

My face shoots in her direction. The question is telling me so much, so much I'm desperate to hear.

"Then why mam; why did you go away? Why are you living in this bloody hovel with a bloke who doesn't give a damn about you?"

She pulls her blanket tighter around herself, so only her head is peeping out. She looks like a swaddled baby ready for bed. Her hair is loose, falling around her face and though she's cold her cheeks are moist with sweat. I've never seen anybody look so ill in my life.

"Liam, I'm too weak to go into it all. I love you and our Pip, and I love your da, just know that for now. I'll explain everything to you when I see you next time I promise, but not tonight. I'm not well and you have to get home."

I don't want to say the obvious, but I must.

"What if we don't get another chance?" I ask flatly.

"Are you coming back?"

I nod.

"Then we'll have another chance."

I must let it go for now because she's struggling to stay awake. She's seen me, so she has hope and she can get stronger. This might not be the last time I see her after all. I'm mad at myself for stewing in my own self-pity for so long and not coming here before tonight.

I wipe my nose with the back of my hand. I'm crying again; I'm crying for Pip, for me, for my father, but mainly for her. So, help me in all my born days did I think I'd feel love and pity for my mother ever again.

Without another thought I pull the stool to perch beside her chair and lean against her chest. Her hand comes out from under the blanket to stroke my hair like she used to do to get me to sleep. If it wasn't for her bony frame and unfamiliar scent, I could almost believe I'm back in the cottage and she's soothing me after a nightmare. She was the best mother in the world once, perhaps she still is, I can't be sure anymore.

"Come back and see me soon, son," she whispers.

"I will," I say.

"Promise me."

"I promise, mam."

Foster will be on his way home by now I should think but I'd prefer not to get up from this stool. If I get up, I'll have to go back to reality because I know even if I can carry her back home this very night, whichever way I turn there will be no waking from this nightmare.

Chapter 17
1892 - Pip

"Check mate," Jarvis says, grinning like the farmer's cat who stole the cream.

My father tuts and rolls his eyes saying, "That was a sideswipe, lad. Cunning some might say, I didn't see it coming. You must have had a good teacher because I haven't beaten you in three nights on the trot."

Jarvis nods rolling his neck this way and that to release the tension. It was a long, tense game, with plenty of banter about who exactly is the best player and why.

"You're right, I did have a good teacher. Old Sid, my dad was a skilled chess player; he learnt from his own father. I've got a chess set at home that's looking a bit worse for wear. Not like this." He picks up a piece, running his forefinger over the face of the king. "Where did you get this set?" he asks.

There's a long silence where I glance over at my father. He won't be comfortable blowing his own trumpet.

"My da whittled it from a leftover piece of ash from the workshop," I tell Jarvis proudly like I did it myself.

"No, you're having me on," he says looking between me and the king piece, "look at the detail on his face, he's even got eyebrows for goodness' sake."

We laugh when he shakes his head, not quite believing us. I can't blame him because it is hard to believe my father could produce such work.

"You don't learn a craft for over forty years and not get half-decent at it," he says modestly.

He stretches his long arms and yawns. He could do with a haircut; it's been a while. His steely hair is curling around his collar and his ears. I'll do it on Sunday after dinner if I remember.

"The snow will start thawing tomorrow and you might be able to get down the valley on Thursday. It'll be gone and forgotten by Thursday night," my father says.

"How can you possibly know that?" Jarvis asks turning the knight piece now in his hand to study it more closely.

"Lad, the same as I know how to whittle a chess piece - years of learning and knowing the season's little signs. It's there for all to see if you care to look. Right then, I'm off up," he says.

The same happened last night and the one before, it's like reliving each day. I've looked forward to my little chats with Jarvis after my father goes to bed. The stories he tells me about what people have been up to in the village and beyond are interesting and eye-opening. He doesn't name names mind, telling me that would be unprofessional. You can tell he's a man who takes his job seriously. I must admit though, over the last few days I've sometimes forgotten why he's here.

I kiss my father's cheek then pack away the chessboard until tomorrow. Perhaps I should ask him to teach me how to play one day. I haven't asked because he used to play with my mother sometimes, and I don't want to be the one to set him off remembering.

"Night, you two," he says now, pulling down his braces on the way to the stairs.

"Goodnight," Jarvis and I say in chorus. We join a low laugh in chorus too before I stoke the embers for the final blaze of the night. The room will stay warm for a couple of hours.

"Are you sitting down at long last then," Jarvis says, nodding to my chair.

It was my mother's chair before mine, but I didn't sit in it until my father made a joke one night and said it would get mice living in it if nobody sat in it. I think it was worse just looking at an empty seat and after six months he must have just decided he couldn't do it any longer. Now we've grown used to it. That's what happens when you do something long enough, you get used to it he told me once when I thought I'd never get over my mother not being here with us.

"If you accept something you can't change, you keep putting one foot in front of the other until you don't exactly get over it, but you get used to it," he said.

He was right, but then he's been right about many things.

Jarvis is watching me intently as I flop into the chair. He still does this often I've noticed, carefully studying my body language. I'm clearly still a suspect.

How he could think I would murder my own mother is beyond me, but then I don't live in his world.

He looks away quickly when I catch his eye.

"This book isn't bad," he says in a strange voice, picking *Jane Eyre* up from the side table, "It's not my usual fare, but there's plenty of intrigue and atmosphere."

I laugh kindly, saying, "Quite the reviewer, Inspector Blackburn. Unfortunately, none of the books in this house are probably your normal fare. Da isn't much of a reader, and Liam spends too much time at the pub or with Sarah to read anymore. I'd say my upbringing made sure we're what you might call 'well-read' though and I'll always be grateful for that."

The omission of who the books belonged to has the same effect of me saying it out loud; I can tell my mother still sits in the middle of both our thoughts.

"*Jane Eyre* is possibly my favourite book," I say, "that or perhaps *Sense and Sensibility*."

He downturns his lips and nods, looking quite impressed, I think.

"Not *Pride and Prejudice* or *Wuthering Heights* then?" he asks.

"Do you know them?" I answer his question with a question, a little surprised. I thought you were more a *Police Gazette* sort of reader.

He laughs, "Not at all, I've heard their names mentioned more than the others you like though. I've no time or inclination generally to read."

"What a terrible loss," I say.

He looks down at the book in his hand to see the edges of the pages are well-thumbed by me and Liam and my mother before us. I try not to let my mind wander to the nights she used to read it to us when we sat in this very room the future thankfully unbeknown.

"This bit made me smile," he says, ""*I would rather be happy than dignified.*""

I can't help but smile too. He went to the exact page so he must have remembered it. Perhaps that's the policeman in him coming out. I liked that sentence when I read it too, thinking at the time that dignity has always been part of my person and sometimes a little silliness surely wouldn't go amiss.

"Do you think you'll always live here, Pip?" he asks suddenly.

Up until now he's only ever called me Miss Metcalfe or indeed nothing at all. I try not to react as I don't want to draw his attention to it and make him self-conscious. Staring into the fire I think about his question.

"I've never thought about it much to be honest, but yes as you ask, I wouldn't mind. Like I said, the main reason is I prefer to be anonymous."

I remember how I could feel all the eyes of the villagers upon me as I walked down the lane in Ackley. We were always the talk of the village even before all this drama.

"Why exactly do you think that is though?" he asks me quietly.

Is this all part of his enquiries, is he trying to see if I'll drop my defences as a prelude to a thorough interrogation at the police station? If he is, it doesn't feel much like it.

Another quote from my favourite book appears. Sometimes you never think about something until the matter is raised and now, I've decided it is my favourite book after our discussion:

"I am no bird; and no net ensnares me: I am a free human being with an independent will."

Blushing, I glance his way realising he's been waiting for an answer, his eyes never leaving my face. I see he's deep in thought.

"I think it's because I don't like to be looked at, especially by people who don't know me, it makes me uncomfortable. Here, I'm free to be who I am. My mother was the same.

A small gasp escapes me—I had no intention of bringing her into the conversation. My defences seem to have dropped away without me knowing.

His Adam's apple is manically bobbing up and down his throat and he's the one who looks to be floundering now. I don't think he knows what to say and neither do I. My mother is the reason he's here in the first place, I'd forgotten for a whisper of a second and now I've brought our minds back to the harsh reality with a thud.

He draws breath as though to speak but then stops. I can only wait to see if he will change his mind as I've no idea how to fill the silence. I drop my eyes, hoping we don't have to wait too long.

"I think she would be very proud of how well you look after your family," he says finally.

When I glance up into his brown eyes, they're warm, glistening in the light of the lowering fire. I can almost see what he's thinking and what he just said was the absolute truth. I'm suddenly pleased my defences have disappeared if only for a while.

For once, I'm not in the least bit uncomfortable under the gaze of a stranger.

And I think perhaps I shall be a little disappointed when the snow starts to thaw tomorrow.

Chapter 18
1892 - Jarvis

I watch Pip and Charlie through the small window of my office door. They're waiting for me, eyes scrolling up and down the corridor, never settling so they look like the guiltiest 'visitors' to ever set foot in the police station. They had to come here, it's only right, and more importantly it's the law, but for once I'm not so keen on it.

I've been home to see ma and to spruce myself up. Some sleep wouldn't have gone amiss after a few nights sleeping in a chair, but there was no time for that.

"Well, I was beginning to think I'd never see you again," she said laughing when I walked in, "thank goodness young Rodge called by to say where you'd gone. I've been worried sick. That place might as well be another country in bad weather. Lord knows how that family put up with it."

That's a fair description, I thought, it was as though I'd crossed an ocean to a different culture and climate. The weather aside, everything was different to home, the mentality, the food, the approach to life. I'm not sure there's anything much to put up with out there though. I miss it already.

My bedroom seemed unfamiliar on my return and even sitting at the table having a sandwich with ma was odd.

I came straight to the station after a bite to eat and I'm due to interview Pip while Mr Douglas will interview Charlie, going over the same questions, but formally for the record and under oath. Both have been warned that anything they say may be taken down and used in evidence. Charlie shrugged at that; Pip looked like a rabbit caught in a snare.

In my heart, I know it's both a waste of time and resources, but nobody can just take my word for it. Protocol must be followed to the letter of course, just like any other case.

Rodge has paid a visit to Sarah Morton's and her father and Liam are coming in to give a statement, little good it will do. Everybody has an alibi of sorts; nothing can be proven or disproven, and I will still be left chasing my tail.

Charlie giving a statement here is bad enough, but seeing Pip in the mire doesn't sit well at all. A police station is no place for a girl like her and I vow to get her out of here as quickly as possible.

I made sure I am the one doing the questioning.

Rodge scribbles away while she answers the questions I've already asked, her shawl carefully folded inside the basket at her feet. Her blonde hair is in a tight bun rather than splayed over her shoulders so I can see every muscle of her face and neck working as she speaks slowly and quietly. Her legs are underneath the interview desk so I can only see the cream bodice of her dress which makes her appear as though she's wearing a nightgown. She looks like a frightened child and I'm so keen for this turmoil to be over for me but especially for her.

I'm especially keen because all the while she sits here, I'm painfully aware she's a bereaved young woman still waiting for her mother to be buried.

Six days in total I stayed with the Metcalfe's, and I'd be lying if I said I hadn't been changed by the experience. I can't tell yet if this will only be temporary like when I went to see a mother whose son had been trampled to death by a horse and cart. When I took her home after she'd seen him lying there, gone forever, I swore to myself I'd never moan about anything again and I meant it.

Yet I did.

Whatever happens though, I'll not forget my last night with the family in a hurry.

The atmosphere lay heavy in the cottage, I could feel it in my bones. Everything had changed; we'd bonded yet nobody could speak of it. I was in the middle of a murder investigation, and though we had no control about how the bond had come about, the situation felt so wrong when returning to real life was imminent.

In the afternoon I'd helped Charlie finish off the beautiful barley twist dresser he was making in the workshop, great slabs of snow sliding off the roof as it thawed. Each dropping slab was a step closer to returning to Ackley. I should have been looking forward to seeing ma, seeing Ivy even as I knew they'd have been wondering where I was.

Throughout my time at *Sunnyside,* I'd discovered so much about Charlie and Pip. Things like how their routine is etched in stone which is why the household runs like clockwork. They make it look easy when they're working so hard.

Pip was making scones when we went inside the house for tea, and I wondered if it was because I happened to mention in passing that they were my favourite. I could scarcely credit that she could be so thoughtful. The peace I'd found eluded me that night as I didn't like the thought of leaving the new way of life I'd found behind. Life was due to return to normal, but I didn't feel anywhere near it.

I first noticed the change in atmosphere as we ate our meal. We were all quiet, pensive almost and Charlie never mentioned a game of chess. I was relieved and disappointed all at once—I would have liked to have seen that magnificent chess set one last time if nothing else.

Charlie went up to bed, and not long afterwards Pip said she was ready to turn in too. The silence between us had become uneasy for the first time because we had so much to say but we knew we shouldn't say it. When she got up from her chair I almost panicked, I just couldn't let the night end.

Then I did something so unlike me—I reached for her hand to stop her leaving.

Normally I'm so careful about how I behave. Even if I'm feeling one way, I can act another. I've always been good at it, and it's been a useful trait to have in my job. That was the moment I realised normality had gone, making me panic more. I held my breath to see what she would do.

She was so alarmed her eyes were like saucers when she looked down at me. She stared into my eyes for too long, but she didn't pull her hand away. She had on a dress I'd never seen before with white daisies on a dark blue background, and it showed off her blonde hair. Each daisy was slightly different as she'd embroidered them herself and I thought of her sitting head bent by the fire, patiently creating each flower to turn a simple dress into a beautiful work of art. I hadn't seen it before, and it was like she'd made a special effort for our little farewell.

"Would you like to go outside to see the last of the snow?" she asked.

The request was strange and unexpected. But I did want to go outside and sit with her as one in the snowy moorland. I might never do it again I thought.

We donned our coats in continued silence, sharing the odd glance. It was like we were heading off on some great unexpected adventure together, both excited yet full of trepidation.

The blast of cold night air should have brought me to my senses and stopped me doing something I knew I shouldn't be doing.

Instead, we tramped to the front of the cottage, both glancing up to Charlie's bedroom window. The room was in darkness, and in that fleeting moment, I've never been more thankful of anything. We walked for about ten minutes with only the faint outline of a path beneath the lowering carpet of white snow as our guide. Did Pip know where we were headed, I wondered; had she thought about doing it all day, perhaps even longer but didn't have the nerve until that moment when I stopped her leaving? I found myself hoping that was the case.

It was so quiet it was as if a whisper might wake the world and give away our secret. We weren't doing anything wrong, yet it felt like we were. I should have been freezing, but I wasn't ... so many contradictions were making me feel like I wasn't myself.

I could hear the stream before I saw it, freeing itself drop by drop from its frozen slumber, the sound drawing us. On the bank I looked down and then back at Pip in awe—the sight that met us was breath-taking; the moon sparkling on the water, the snow carrying the light further, so it looked never-ending.

She was smiling, enjoying my pleasure, but unfazed and I realised then she had seen it before at this time of night. Uncoiling my scarf, I laid it on a patch of snowless grass for us to sit on. It was folded so short in length, it meant we had to sit very close together. It felt good to have her so near me, enjoying such a special place. I now think of it as our special place.

How many times have you been here at this hour?" I whispered.

Her head was turned away from me as she said, "Only once. I ran out into the night when I thought my sobs were going to choke me. I'd held them inside until I couldn't any longer after ... after my mother left. I couldn't risk upsetting Liam and da, so I pulled my coat over my nightdress and ran and ran until I found here. It was waiting for me."

Oh Pip, I thought then, you of everyone I'd ever met do not deserve to have such pain. You only give expecting nothing in return. Reaching for her hand in her mitten, we sat a while just the two of us, me trying to stem the tears which were threatening to come. The last time I'd cried was when dad died. All that day my feelings had been swimming too close to the surface, scaring the living daylights out of me.

I don't know how long it was before she finally turned to look at me, it could have been minutes or hours, but it didn't matter as I would have sat there until dawn. When I saw her beautiful face, I knew I wanted to kiss her, and not just to try and take the pain away. I wanted to kiss her so I could take part of her away with me when I had to leave. She leaned towards me, and I met her in the middle to touch lips so gently, so tenderly a felt a tear finally escape to hurtle down my cheek. I was peaceful yet my heart was racing, a feeling I'd never had before in my entire life, like so many others.

We walked back to the cottage together, my arm around her shoulders, hers around my waist until we got to the door at the side. I looked down at her for so long before I kissed her for what would be the last time, this time our lips were more searching, so I had a powerful stirring in the pit of my stomach, a longing that became a sign on my lips.

"I don't want to leave you," I whispered, "I don't want to go home; those few miles may as well be all the way to the moon."

She pulled away to stare at me.

"Oh, Jarvis, I'd hate you to lose your job because of me. We're skating on such thin ice here and we both know it," she said.

I shook my head dismissively, unsure if I felt the same way when only days before my job was my life.

"Will you be alright?" I asked.

Touching my cheek, she smiled shyly up at me.

"As right as you will be," she said.

She knew. She felt the same as I did.

I didn't know if I'd be alright.

I still don't know now.

*

I question Liam further and Ken Morton corroborates his story to Mr Douglas that he was drinking with Liam at the *Rose & Crown* on the evening in question and then they'd gone back to stay at his house like he does often when they've had a few too many. There have been no surprises, everything has turned out as I expected.

Ken has left us to go home, and Liam has gone to reunite with his father and sister. I watch him hugging Pip, both with their eyes closed and then shake his father's hand, putting his other hand on his shoulder and leaning towards him. They are a family who are bonded by tragedy but also by love and respect.

It takes me a while to turn away from the scene but when I do, I've come to a decision. I head to Mr Douglas's room and knock on the door. I have an important question, one which may give the family a chance to move forward.

On my return, they're all sitting in a row in my office waiting for me, Pip in the middle, a white rose between two thorns, I think. Except Charlie and Liam are no thorns I've discovered, they're two good, hardworking men.

For once I'm aware of the state of my office, seeing it with their eyes, papers piled, so Mrs Morris the cleaner moans she can never give anything a good going over. Tidiness has always been the last on my list of priorities when it comes to my job but it's not a room fit for visitors.

"I won't keep you long," I say spotting the dust particles swimming around our heads in the winter sunlight, "I have news I wanted to tell you myself. First though, I'd like to thank you for your hospitality over the last week, you couldn't have made me more welcome, particularly under the circumstances."

My eyes look anywhere but at Pip, but it was something that needed to be said.

"Ay, well, you didn't give us any bother," Charlie says making us all snort. We're all too pent up to have any chance at laughing freely.

"Right, so, I've spoken to my chief inspector, and I can inform you that the postmortem has been completed and the coroner has opened and adjourned the inquest, pending further enquiries by the police. So, they will now release the body for burial. You can make arrangements for the funeral as you are still her next of kin of course."

Charlie and Liam's hands come out together to cover each of Pip's. She's surrounded by love and that's some consolation, I think. Her eyes are on the floor when I tear rolls down her cheek, and I shuffle some papers on my desk to distract me from having to look at it.

"That's good of you to tell us in person, Inspector Blackburn," Charlie says, "now if you don't mind, I think we'd like to get back before it gets dark."

"Of course," I say quietly, somehow wishing I could jump aboard that cart outside and join them by their fireside if only for one last time.

We say our farewells and Pip nods her head in my direction, her eyes only fleetingly looking into mine. It's long enough to see the desolation staring back at me.

And as they leave me for the long trip home, I sit back down wearily at my desk, put my head in my hands and let out a long breath.

The only thought I have in my mind now is a vow to cull that bloody thorn also known as Bradley Foster. I'll make sure he gets what's coming to him if it's the last thing I do on this earth.

Chapter 19
1892 - Pip

I spot him first. Jarvis is stood side by side with Chief Inspector Douglas and the sergeant—I forget his name—as I turn around. They've all made a special effort to look extra smart for the occasion and it briefly touches me they should go to so much trouble on our behalf.

I turn quickly back to my mother's grave. Standing by my mother's grave is not something I thought I would be doing for years, not until I was about thirty-five, thirty at least. She's too young and so am I.

There are only the six of us including three policemen in attendance which must surely be the poorest turnout in Ackley for a funeral. I'm thankful Bradley Foster clearly knew what was good for him and stayed away today. He'll not want to be under the watchful eye of the police but then he's damned if he does and damned if he doesn't attend the funeral, people will point the finger either way. I'm relieved he's not here though as I perish the thought of what our Liam might have said to him … or done to him. It's been keeping me awake at night because the last thing we need on our plate is our Liam getting into any bother.

With good intentions, I've always found it impossible to concentrate on what the reverend is preaching at the best of times. We used to come to church occasionally when my mother was at home, but my father never mentioned it afterwards and Liam and I aren't really worried either way. At least it gave the villagers a real reason to think we were odd in not doing whatever anybody else does on a Sunday morning. I was past caring by then as all I could think about was how to get my mother back home.

The church service before the burial was brief. I only listened intently when Reverend Phillips spoke about my mother and her life back in Ireland. I suspect he didn't really want to do the service, more than likely considering us a family of heathens, but he wouldn't have had any choice in the matter as a man of the cloth.

He came out to the cottage last week and had tea with us by the fire like he came visiting all the time. My father told him what he knew which was mostly what I knew already, but then he mentioned the names of my mother's parents and my ears pricked: Blaithin and Declan. I had to ask him later which way round they were as I'd never heard the names before. I don't know why I didn't know, but I suppose they were always just granny and grandpa when my mother talked about them, and she did that a lot. They were both on her mind for very different reasons.

The one thing new I discovered from the reverend was that Orla means 'Golden Princess' in Irish. It's so fitting for her, and I was only glad I was far too nervous to cry when he told us.

"Perhaps we'll see you on Sunday, Mr Metcalfe," the reverend said on his way out.

"Ay perhaps, thank you for coming, reverend," my father said, and they looked at each other too long for my liking.

"Dust to dust," Reverend Phillips is saying now, and a handful of soil drops from his unclenched fist onto the coffin.

The noise startles me out of my thoughts, and I can't help letting out an odd noise, half scream, half gurgle. My father grabs my hand and I realise it's shaking like a leaf in the breeze. Oh no, don't cry Pip, I think, don't you cry now, or you'll never be able to stop. Wait until later when you're on your own.

Liam is standing like a soldier on parade to my right, and I take a peek at his face. It's as stiff as the rest of his body but if I take his hand he'll shatter into a million pieces, I know that expression. I'm pleased he's home for the time being at least until he marries Sarah. It will be nice when they can set a date and make a start with the preparations, but it's a shame they'll be planning a wedding with a cloud like this hanging over them. I think Sarah and her parents might have come to the funeral today if they could have taken time off from the mill. They've never tarred us with the same brush as everyone else around here.

Everyone in Ackley will be taking bets about who killed my mother, it'll be all they talk about down the pub and in the shop. I can hear them now discussing how old Charlie had an axe to grind after she left him for another bloke. Mind you, they'll say, that Bradley Foster is a nasty piece of work, it could just as well have been him. I only hope Liam doesn't overhear their gossip or they'll all be sorry.

These are far from the thoughts I should be having in the middle of my mother's funeral, but I suppose it's better than the alternative. I'd rather not think of her lying in that coffin all alone in the dark.

I take a gulp of cold air and close my eyes. I can feel Jarvis almost willing me to stay calm, trying his utmost to give me the strength to get through this trauma.

There's a question which has been following me around since he left and it's not one that I can be sure I would know the answer to:

Am I in love?

All I do know is that I miss him terribly and part of me was thinking about seeing him when I was getting ready this morning. The distraction was welcome but then I was ashamed because I should only have been thinking of my mother on her funeral day.

I wonder if he's seen Ivy much since he returned to the village. I wonder if he's slotted back into his old life and one day, in the not-too-distant future he'll ask her to marry him like everyone expects.

That's not a pleasant thought I've realised too late. I knew he was seeing Ivy so what do I expect? He's a policeman and he has a mother and responsibilities, I've no business interfering in all that.

When I wake up on a morning, memories of my mother flood me, but it's not too long before Jarvis swims between them. Was his time living at the cottage even real I often wonder. Some days I think not, but then I remember how he looked at me and how safe I felt when he held my hand by the stream that snowy night.

My father nudges me so I turn and follow obediently behind him. He drops some soil on the coffin without looking down at it. I drop some and watch it fall and crumble over the coffin lid, then I look for Liam but he's not there. He refuses to join us, even when I wave him over. I give up and return to his side to wait for the end of the service. It must be due anytime soon surely.

I don't even notice when Reverend Phillips finally stops talking. My father just pulls me by the hand to walk away and I grab Liam's hand because I know he's still in his own world. I can't help myself glancing over my shoulder to my left.

It would have been better if I hadn't. The look on Jarvis's face is awful, so much so I'm fighting the urge to run and bury my head in his coat lapels to hide until life stops being a living nightmare.

Oh, Phillipa, you're losing all sense of reason now, I scold myself. Not much longer and I'll be back in my rightful place at *Sunnyside*, closing the door on the cold, harsh world for a while until it catches up with me again.

The three policemen follow a short distance behind us as we leave the graveyard. My father is thanking Reverend Phillips for a beautiful service, his voice flat and monotone, and I take the reverend's hand when he offers it. He places his other palm on top as though he's trying to relay his sympathies.

"In time it will get better, my dear," he says kindly, and his eyes are full of compassion, convincing me his words are genuine and it really, truly will get better.

He gives me back some hope, and I take it like a spoonful of medicine.

Bella is waiting patiently by our cart, and we climb aboard to wait for my father to join us. Each of the policemen take off their hats and nod in our direction as they pass by, but they don't say a word.

Jarvis briefly touches Bella's nose as he goes past, and she brays slightly as though she remembers him. We used to go to the stable together to feed her after a couple of days and Jarvis even mucked the stable out one afternoon without me even asking. I think he grew fond of her.

Two men with spades pass my father as he walks towards us, both taking off their cap and bowing their head until he goes by.

"Do you think we're dreaming, Pip?" Liam asks with tears in his eyes as he looks from them to me.

The spades are a reminder I'd much prefer to bury. Taking my brother's hand, I hold it in my lap with both of my own. They're freezing and I gently rub them like I did when he was a little boy.

"One day we'll rise in the morning and get about our day without feeling this weight we're carrying, Liam. One day it will happen, I'm sure of it, otherwise how do people go on?"

I rub his hand harder saying, "I told you to wear your gloves, but would you listen? Oh, no."

Though his smile is sad, it settles me.

Jarvis and the others are standing by the corner shop, lined up tidily on parade, waiting to pay their respects as we go by on the cart.

When da jiggles Bella's reins to gee her up, my heart suddenly starts to pound and I'm not sure why.

The shop doorbell goes, and Mrs Davies comes out to join the line of policemen, wrapping her shawl tighter around herself and hopping from one foot to the other. My heart races faster, faster as we get closer to Jarvis and see he's staring at me with his hat in his hand.

Mrs Davies's pinched face only serves to tell me how sorry she is for me so I can't help but attempt a smile to console her. She does the same, so we are two women leaning on each other, offering sympathy without words. I always had a sense she liked me or had an empathy for me at least and now I know for certain.

Over her shoulder I spot someone staring through the shop window. Ivy is wearing a pink gown with ribbons in her hair to match. The vibrant colour stands out in the sea of black in front of the window, looking odd at such a sad occasion.

But I am a nobody to Ivy, she doesn't acknowledge my existence, never mind the death of my mother. She will have jumped out of bed today to choose her prettiest gown as she does every other day.

Through the glass Ivy's eyes are fixed on Jarvis, whose eyes remain fixed on me, I now notice.

She follows his gaze slowly until her eyes meet mine and lock. My heart is now hammering in my ears and my face lights on fire.

I think that just this minute Ivy Davies has finally acknowledged my existence, but I fear it might have been in my best interests to remain invisible.

Because the look she is giving me in her pretty pink dress is nothing short of withering.

Chapter 20
1892 - Jarvis

"What the blazes …" I shout, charging towards the two men on the ground outside the *Travs*.

I'm worn out, all I want is to go home and fall into bed, that's all I want but apparently, it's too much to ask.

One man is bigger than the other, but the smaller man is giving him a run for his money like a ferocious terrier fired up enough to do some damage. The bigger man is struggling to get to his feet in the kerfuffle because the punches heading his way may not be as powerful but they're relentless.

My heart sinks when I recognise who the men are. It's none other than Foster and Liam going at it hammer and tongs on the rain-soaked pavement, two other men egging them on, fuelling the fire. They're enjoying themselves heckling the show.

I grab Liam's coat collar from behind and pull him off Foster whose nose and top lip are bloodied.

"Get off me," Liam yells trying to wriggle himself free from my grasp, "get your bloody hands off me!"

"Liam, stop it," I say, pushing him up against the pub wall, "get a hold of yourself lad, this won't do you any good will it? Think of your sister, your da, they've got enough to worry about."

Glancing over my shoulder I see Foster getting to his feet.

"He's off his head, he needs locking up. Take him down the station and chuck him in the cells for the night, he's a fecking maniac."

Foster wipes his mouth, leaving a snail's trail of redness on his sleeve.

"You killed her, Foster, I know you did, you bloody well killed her!" Liam shouts, his voice sounding somewhere between a screech and a wail. He pushes my hand away roughly, "You should be locking *him* up. He should be waiting to be hanged by now. Why can't you find any evidence to get him. He beat her, I know it, everyone knows it, that should be enough on its own for Christ's sake."

Liam drops down the wall sobbing. He's had more than a few pints by the look of him which isn't helping matters. Foster is a man who can hold his ale, he's no doubt had plenty of practice. The two drunks have gone back inside the pub, bored now the entertainment for the evening is over.

"They've no proof about that or anything else, Metcalfe," Foster says, buttoning up his jacket then pushing his drenched hair from his face with both hands, "She was frail, she was always falling over, and she bruised easily. Keep your accusations to yourself. It wasn't my pencil they found as evidence now, was it?"

I'm glad to see him backing away as he's setting the record straight. All I care about now is getting Liam sorted out, Foster can get out of my hair for the time being.

I sit in the rain beside Liam. I'm soaked anyway and as ma says, once you're wet, you're wet.

"Look, you can rest assured I'm working my backside off to pin something on him, Liam," I tell him.

I'm well aware I shouldn't be speaking to him at all about the case but how can I leave a man whose mother has been murdered to sit in the gutter and stew?

His face is plastered to his head, the rain running down freely as he turns to me like a little boy lost. I think of Pip at home by the fire with their da and my stomach moves in the way it does every time I think of her. It's like a homesickness.

"Ay, but it's not enough is it. He's in here getting plastered every night and my mam's … my mam's …"

He drops his head to her knees, and I can't help my arm going around his shoulders. Oh, Liam lad, go home to your sister, she'll look after you, I think but I can't say a word.

"Are you staying at Sarah's?" I ask him when he finally lifts his head to wipe a hand across his face. He nods sullenly.

Getting to my feet I hold out my hand. He looks at it a minute then takes it, so I pull him up and straighten his jacket. He picks his cap up from the ground and puts it on, running both palms over his wet cheeks. Then he sets off to walk in the direction of the Morton house.

"I'll come with you," I say.

He looks over his shoulder to give me a smile that makes my throat knot.

"It's alright inspector," he says, "I'm fine now, but thanks, and thanks for not taking me down the station. Anyway, I don't think Sarah's dad would appreciate me bringing the police to his door."

I watch until I see him disappear inside the house then I head towards home. Poor lad, I think, I'm getting more than a little desperate myself about the situation. It's all I think about day and night, but it's like I'm stuck, unable to find a way to move forward. It's not a feeling I'm used to.

At the corner shop I'm startled as somebody appears from around the back of the building out of nowhere. I recognise the silhouette under their umbrella as Ivy—she's been watching it all happening out here from her bedroom I imagine, along with the rest of the street.

"God, look at the state of you," is her welcome, "you look like something the cat dragged in."

I ignore her comment. It will be better all round if I get straight to the point, especially as I want to get to bed.

"I'm sorry I haven't called to see you since I got back, Ivy, but I've been following a lead with the case," I tell her, screwing my eyes up to the rain which is now torrential.

I can't see the expression on her face, but I can picture it well enough.

"Well, that's why I'm here, if you won't come to me, then what's a girl supposed to do?"

She tries to make her tone playful, but she doesn't succeed. I don't know what to say, how to explain, and then her sigh is so dramatic even the sound of the rain can't drown it out.

"Ivy …"

She puts her free hand up, shaking her head.

"You don't need to tell me, I know it's over," she says.

I'm wondering now if I lead her on. If I have it's because ma was so keen for me to settle down with her and I couldn't just man up and tell her straight. I should have told her that Ivy is a beautiful girl with good prospects, but sadly not the girl for me. Pip or no Pip she could never be the girl for me.

"I just wish you could have come to my door and told me yourself, that's all."

She pauses for so long I start to apologise but she talks over me, "I saw how you were looking at that strange Metcalfe girl the other day."

The hairs on the back of my neck tighten; I don't like the term 'strange', especially when she doesn't know the first thing about Pip Metcalfe.

"Ivy, it's true we became friends when I was snowed in at her house, but this isn't about her. I don't think you and I are right for each other if we're being honest with ourselves."

She laughs, but it's not a pleasant sound.

"But you and her *are* right for each other. You've discovered that in a week, I take it," she says, "as far as I was concerned, we were perfectly fine before your little … trip."

"Ivy, you won't be on your own for long, I'm sure there are plenty of suitors waiting in the wings, but …."

"…but you'd rather shack up with the village idiot," she interrupts.

If she had slapped me, she could not have made more of an impact with those words.

"Don't, call her that, don't you ever call her that again!"

There's a silent stand-off, where we throw daggers at each other with the rain hammering her umbrella and the pavement almost deafening. How I want to go home, slam the door and never see this woman again. If only this was even possible. Oh, I'm growing to hate this village now I'm seeing it through different eyes.

"All I know, Inspector Blackburn is this: mother and I think that damn family deserve everything they get!"

With that parting shot she heads back up the ginnel at the side of the shop until she disappears around the back.

I clasp a hand to my wet mouth and bite my lip hard to stop me hurling an insult. My hand is shaking with rage, so it's lucky for Ivy that I've been brought up only to treat a woman with a gentle hand because I've never had it tested before.

But right at this moment I'm hanging onto my self-control by the very skin of my teeth.

Chapter 21
1892 - Pip

Christmas looms large. We didn't think it could get any worse than the first year after my mother left, when we tried to pretend it was just another day. At the eleventh hour we went along with my father's request to make an effort, forcing the festivities until I went to bed on Christmas night with a headache to end all others.

Only five days left to go, and it will be upon us once more.

Faking a festive mood this time is too much for us we've decided, but we're to have a proper Christmas dinner at least and Liam is to join us, weather permitting. He's toing and froing to Sarah's and the pub, yomping miles or riding Bella if it's decent underfoot, and still putting in the hours with da in the workshop. I've been wondering of late if he can't allow himself to stop in case his mind catches up with him.

"Are you ready, lass?" my father asks, pulling his big coat on over his overalls.

I feel a little queasy as I nod and put the guard over the fire. We're heading into Ackley to buy everything except the goose which is on order for Liam to collect on Christmas Eve. He's pushing the boat out he told us, and he'll not have any complaints from us.

However, this means I must go to the shop and risk running into Ivy yet again. She definitely knows something, though I'm not even sure myself what that something could be.

Mrs Davies is pleasant enough when she sees me, but then we're one of her best customers so she has no alternative. Ivy always comes into the shop from the back nowadays on the pretext of fetching some random item or other, but she only wants to make me uncomfortable. How much Ivy knows is a mystery as I haven't seen Jarvis since the day of the funeral.

"You've been a bit quiet love," my father says as we jostle along on the cart, "I know we've had a miserable time of it of late, but I hope you'd tell me if there was anything else on your mind."

I know he's fishing. He's not daft, so he'll have noticed the way Jarvis looked at me at the funeral or even before then when he was staying with us. No good can come of it all though, so I think it best to keep my powder dry.

"I'm alright da, don't worry about me. This Christmas was always going to be the worst, we knew that."

We glance at each other and share a sad smile. His expression makes me feel like a hand is squeezing my heart.

"But once we get it over and done with, we can start the new year afresh."

Oh da, for me the bleakness of January is looming just as much. Where once I was happy being cut off with the weather, now it will only give me more time to fill my thoughts. Jarvis will seem further away than he does already.

I push the thought away and a comfortable silence descends as I take in the view of the frost-covered hills. Some may wonder why I never tire of this landscape, but it's because it's ever-changing, a new living painting to look at every single day.

My heart skips a beat when we turn onto the lane and spot a man in a familiar black overcoat, his brass buttons gleaming as he waits a few doors down from the shop entrance. He takes off his hat as we approach, and my father pulls Bella to stop.

"Mr Metcalfe, Miss Metcalfe," he says inclining his head slightly, "I've been waiting for you to come to the village for your provisions. I have some news and I wondered if you might accompany me to the station. There's nothing to worry about, so please don't alarm yourself."

That phrase, "nothing to worry about" rarely bodes well in my experience. My father and I exchange brief glances, and I can tell he's thinking along the same lines as me.

"Hello, Inspector Blackburn," my father says with forced cheeriness, "I hope this means you finally have an update on the case, it would be the best Christmas present for us this year. Jump on, we might as well ride to the station together to save horseshoes."

Jarvis climbs aboard the cart to sit by my side. I'm wedged firmly between him and my father, so his thigh is tight against mine. He's no near, I can hear his shallow breaths and I try and concentrate on the road ahead.

What is it he's discovered I wonder, and will it be what I want to know? Our shoulders gently tap together as we ride along the uneven cobbles. All eyes are upon us behind the lace curtains, I know it, they're almost burning me as we pass each window one by one.

I'm thankful to arrive at the station and Jarvis instructs my father to go through the open gates and around the back. When we come to a standstill, he jumps from his seat to help me down and my palm slides into his open hand. Even with the barrier of wool and cloth, I can feel him as intensely as the night by the stream. I've yet to look at him.

The police sergeant glances up as we enter, nodding his head by way of greeting.

"It's parky out there, Sergeant Rogerson. Three cups of tea if you wouldn't mind," Jarvis says.

Ah Rogerson, that's his name.

"Yes sir," he responds, jumping up from his seat to get to the task immediately.

We follow behind Jarvis as we go into his room, and he takes off his hat to hang it on the rack by the door. He gestures with his hand for us to take the two seats opposite him on the other side of his desk.

As I sit down next to my father I'm still shivering from cold and fear of the unknown, unable yet to feel the benefit of the fire.

"Well, I've been busy since last we met," Jarvis says, "and you're quite right, Mr Metcalfe, I've discovered some information which has finally nudged the case forward I believe."

I look at my father, but his mind is racing ahead of me.

"That is good news, inspector. What exactly have you found out?" he says, never one to beat about the bush and I notice Jarvis can't help the shadow of a smile.

My patience wanes for once when Sergeant Rogerson appears with a tray of teacups. All the while he's fussing with our refreshments, I want him to leave so I can find out what Jarvis has uncovered for us. He takes a long swig from his mug while my father and I leave ours where they are on the desk.

"I've received word from colleagues in County Donegal, Ireland," he pauses to look at us in turn, "but I must advise you that it's not news you will want to hear I'm afraid. You must prepare yourselves for quite a shock. I doubt you will know what I'm about to disclose, Mr Metcalfe."

Oh, not more shocks, how many more can a person take? I'm sick to the back teeth of them. I blow my tea to cool it and take a long gulp.

"Are you alright with your daughter being here?" Jarvis asks.

My father looks at me and I nod to make his decision for him. I'm not going anywhere, and woe betide anyone who tries to insist right at this moment.

Jarvis clears his throat, looking at the light beige folder on his desk. I try to read the upside-down writing on the front.

"What did you know about your wife's previous life in Ireland?" he asks.

My father cocks his head, shrugging once.

"As much as she told me, which is all I could know. Why?"

Jarvis opens the file then slides a small head and shoulders photograph of a man across the desk.

My father and I look at each other before leaning over the desk together to take a good look.

Underneath the photograph of the man is a blackboard which clearly states the name Brendan Ferguson and the number 62791.

My father picks the photograph up and studies it. I don't need to study it; I'm certain already the photograph is of none other than the man we know as Bradley Foster.

I quickly stir three spoons of sugar into my father's tea and hand it to him. I must nudge him twice before he takes it from me and then again for him to have a drink.

"Why are you showing me this?" he asks.

I reach for his hand to prepare us for what's coming, as surely as day follows night. I glance sideways at my father; all colour drained from his face enough to concern me.

"We've discovered that Mrs Metcalfe was previously married. Were you aware of this fact?"

My father's free hand goes to his mouth. I squeeze his hand and try to understand what Jarvis is telling us. It must be true because he wouldn't be telling us if he wasn't absolutely certain. How could we not know his wife, my mother had a husband before?

"No, I'm afraid I wasn't aware of that," he whispers.

Jarvis turns to look at me, his eyes wide with concern. I look away before I crumple backwards into the chair, still unable to let go of my father's hand.

"I see," Jarvis says, "well then, this brings me to my next point: I'm sorry to tell you we have been unable to locate any divorce documentation. It appears your … your wife is… er was still married to this man, Brendan Ferguson," he points to the photograph.

My father has snatched his hand away and jumped out of his chair before I've even had time to process what on god's green earth Jarvis Blackburn is getting at.

I push a hand to my chest.

I've finally grasped the implication behind his words, and now I only wish that I hadn't.

Chapter 22
1892 - Pip

"Pip, I will not ask you again, please move to one side," Jarvis says.

Though my legs are threatening to give way, I stay planted firmly to the spot, tears mixing with the snow falling on my face.

"I can't, I just can't, I must come with you, or I'll walk to his house, and you might find me buried in the snow. Please, Jarvis, you must understand how I feel. We're wasting time … please."

My final plea spurs him into action. Oh, the relief, it washes over me. But it's only seconds before the fear returns to swaddle me.

He flings himself from King, his police horse to help me up and then scrabbles back aboard to sit in front of me. Instinctively I wrap my arms around his waist as he pulls the reins for King to start our journey. Jarvis barely looks left and right down the street for anyone passing before he takes us almost immediately to a full gallop. My bonnet drops backwards to rest on my shoulders, but I don't notice until the wetness of the snow chills my scalp. There's no need to tell him to go faster as I can feel his sense of urgency even through his jacket, his heart pounding, the muscles of his thighs working overtime to make us fly as fast and furious as the wind.

My father had stormed out of the station without so much as a bye your leave, so Jarvis and I could only stare agog after him, wasting precious seconds. It was obvious once we'd pulled ourselves together where he was heading but by the time Jarvis had scrabbled into his coat to go outside, the cart was standing alone, and my father was already hurtling on Bella towards the moors.

All the while Jarvis was shouting over his shoulder for me to stay where I was, I was instead running to keep up with him. I followed him to the stable where the boy who tended the police horses was told bluntly to step to one side by Jarvis then he climbed aboard King.

"I'm coming with you," I said in a panic.

He didn't look at me, saying, "Pip, I know you're beside yourself, but this is police business. Please, you must wait here until we get back."

Before he had chance to leave the stable, I ran in front of King and blocked the pathway at the side of the station. It wasted even more time, but I had to go with him come what may. I would not negotiate so here I am sitting on the back of a police horse and climbing the moors to take a short cut to the cottage my mother shared with the man who now appears to be her husband.

I mustn't think about that, all that matters is stopping my father taking the law into his own hands, because I cannot lose him to the noose. He and Liam are my world, and I will do whatever is necessary to prevent this happening. My father will listen to me more than Jarvis, I have a better chance of making him see reason. My arms tighten around Jarvis, and I bury my head into the back of his coat. Oh please, don't let us be too late. My father is not, has never been a violent man, but we find ourselves in extraordinary circumstances. The most extraordinary of circumstances.

I finally spot the barn over Jarvis's shoulder and see Bella untethered outside the front door. The barn door is half open but I'm still clinging to the hope Bradley Foster, Brendan Ferguson or whoever the man is, isn't at home. Even while we're slowing to a trot to approach, I know I'm clutching at straws. It's a Saturday teatime, so he won't be working, and he'll be back from the lunchtime session at the pub. I imagine my father descending unexpectedly on a drunken Brendan Ferguson and perish the thought.

I can hear raised voices from the top of the path. When we finally come to a stop, Jarvis makes one last-ditch attempt to ask me to stay on the horse, but he must catch me before I fall by the time he's finished pleading.

He's running now and I'm keeping pace, pure nervous energy driving me on.

We step inside and although they glance our way, my father doesn't even acknowledge our presence. He's gone to another place, a place I've not seen before.

"You followed her here to make her life a misery and that of her family," he's yelling,

"Have you any idea what you've done man … have you?"

My father takes a step towards Ferguson.

"Da, don't he's not worth hanging for!" I scream, "Don't leave me like my mother did for *him*!"

I make to run towards him, but Jarvis pulls me back by my arm. My father spins around, his face so contorted with rage I'm terrified by it.

His jaw hangs when he sees my expression, his face now softening so he looks like my father once more.

"Pip, you shouldn't have come here. Blackburn, why did you let her come and see this?"

Jarvis lets go of my arm and I place a tentative hand on my father's shoulder, half wondering if he'll shrug it off. When I feel his shoulder sag under my fingers I want to weep with relief.

Ferguson is glancing between all of us, looking like a shabby mess of a man with wild hair, and a jumper covered with stains. He disgusts me. I have one eye on him the whole time, knowing Jarvis will be doing the same.

"Where else would I be, da? I can't risk losing you too, I had to try and stop you."

My father turns his head to meet his nemesis eye to eye.

"This man has no shame or regret for what he's done. We're not dealing with a normal person, he's a cold, calculating murderer. Liam knew it and now I know it in my heart to be true. You killed my wife, her mother, Liam's mother. You killed her and the world and his wife know it and now you'll pay for it."

Jarvis now steps in between the men as I put my arm around my father's shoulder just to be sure he isn't tempted to act on impulse.

"He will Charlie, but that's my job," Jarvis says coolly taking command of the situation. My face flying in his direction grows hot.

"Confess, Ferguson. The game's up, we know you beat Mrs Metcalfe, she had enough bruises on her to tell a story, even without everything else we found. You must have really hated her for leaving you all those years ago and when you found out she'd got another family that must have tipped you over the edge," Jarvis says levelly.

Ferguson suddenly sits down heavily at the table as if Jarvis's words have taken the very breath from him.

I can't look at that table, it brings back too many horrid memories, so I just stare at the man I've now grown to despise.

"Yes, I hated her," he snaps, making no effort to conceal his Irish accent any longer, "and maybe I was a little loose with my hands from time to time but—and this is a very big but—I swear on all that's holy I didn't kill her and I'm not going to let you pin it on me when I didn't do it!"

Are these weaselly words from an inveterate liar and bully who feels the noose tightening? Perhaps, but there's something about his manner and the despair in his voice that doesn't fit. I can't deny what he's saying, there's a world of difference between hitting someone and murdering them and as I look to my father and Jarvis, it's clear they are thinking the same.

There's only circumstantial evidence against him and they can't even get him on bigamy charges; it was my mother who was the bigamist. I feel sick at the realisation.

"She must have had a good reason to run away from you and flee her home in Ireland," I hear myself saying, "what did you do to her?"

Pushing his chair back from the table he stands to his full height, so Jarvis and my father instinctively do the same. Jarvis is a similar height whereas my father is about half a foot smaller.

"It's funny you should ask that, *miss*," Ferguson says, with a sarcastic emphasis on the 'miss', "we might not have seen eye to eye over there, but she did have a particular reason for taking the boat across the sea when she did."

The sound of my own breathing fills my head and I'm licking my lips manically waiting for what he will no doubt take great pleasure in telling us.

"It might interest you to know your mam was having a kid when she left me," he says, turning his attention from me to my father, "isn't that right Charlie?" he asks, his eyes mocking.

Everything becomes a blur now: my father swerves around Jarvis to lunge at Ferguson and grabs him by the throat. I'm pulling my father back from behind with every ounce of strength I can muster until Jarvis gets his arms around my waist to lift me out of the way. Then he puts himself between the two men who are clearly hell bent on killing one another. There is a scrum of arms and legs and it's impossible to tell what's going on.

My father finally frees himself to throw a punch and the sound is loud and sickening as it connects with Ferguson's jaw. Ferguson is knocked clean off his feet like a doll that's been thrown across the floor. I see him fall against the fender on the hearth as if in slow motion, and now I'm rushing to stand next to my father to wait for Ferguson to get to his feet. His retaliation will be brutal I fear but I'll not let him get close enough to my da, not in a million years. I stand tall like a warrior all set for battle to commence.

Except now only a silence swamps us. Ferguson doesn't get to his feet, in fact, Ferguson remains on the floor and doesn't move a muscle.

We all watch on as a pool of blood appears from underneath his head and trickles between the stone flags of the floor before disappearing.

Then we all watch on as the light is snuffed from Brendan Ferguson's eyes, and somehow, I already know the light has gone out of them ... for good.

Chapter 23
Jarvis - 1892

"I'm sorry, Blackburn but you are to be suspended from duty with immediate effect."

The words ring in my ears and with them the memory of Chief Inspector Douglas's disappointed expression hits me clean between the eyes and makes my stomach drop to my boots.

"Jarvis, get yourself down here for breakfast, you can't hide in your room all day, lad!"

Ma's voice travels up the stairs well enough and I pull the covers over my head. I came home after the meeting feeling like a wrung-out rag, but ma took one look at my face, and I knew there was no chance of just slinking under the bedcovers.

I learned as a young boy there's no use twisting the truth with ma for two reasons: one, she's sharp as a tack and two, the truth will always come out in this village one way or another.

"Tell me everything," she said, "and don't bother leaving anything out or I'll know."

My eyes felt like they were in the back of my head I was so tired. Ma had her rags in her hair, with a cup of warm milk on the side table waiting to take up to bed. The last remaining flickering candles of the tree in the window took me by surprise, I'd almost forgotten it was Christmas.

I was cornered. Raising my eyes to heaven, I decided she deserved to hear the truth, however uncomfortable it might be for me.

"You remember when I was snowed in at the Metcalfe's?"

She shook her head dismissively, already irritated by my delaying tactics in asking the obvious.

"Well, as you can imagine it was an intense week. The three of us were obviously thrown together twenty-four hours a day in close proximity and …" I paused wondering how to phrase my assessment of the situation.

"… and you fell in love with Pip Metcalfe," ma said, knocking me sideways with her intuition. I admit it was a relief not to have to say the words aloud. I couldn't have put it better myself.

"You never cease to amaze me, ma. How did you guess?" I asked.

She put her feet up in turn on the footstool then laid back in her chair, arms folded, set to stay right where she was for a while.

"Jarvis, if a mother doesn't know the bones of her own child, then she's fallen short."

Ma's thoughts on the Metcalfe family are more compassionate than the rest of the villagers. However, Ivy was her number one choice of girl for me, so I can't imagine the realisation had been sitting well.

"Have you told Ivy yet?" she asked, only confirming my suspicions.

I nodded and she sighed, leaning her head on the back of the chair.

"I haven't told her about my feelings for Pip, I wanted to let her down gently. In any case, we're just not suited though I tried to see past it for you more than anybody."

"Well, that was a daft thing to do, don't you think? She may have been top of my list, but you've got a tongue in your head. You should have said you weren't that struck on her."

"I know, but you were so keen, and I didn't know the difference until I met Pip," I paused, "but the thing is, Ivy came to the station tonight to tell Mr Douglas about my feelings for Pip and now I'm up to my neck in hot water."

Her face turning puce, ma sat bolt upright in her seat, legs akimbo, a look of horror on her face.

"She did what? She never did surely, I can't believe she would be so nasty and underhand," she said.

I wasn't quite so astonished to be having the conversation with Mr Douglas, Ivy is no shrinking violet when it comes to getting her own way.

"Hell hath no fury like a woman scorned, they say and I've made the situation worse because I should have declared my feelings for a murder suspect by rights. I haven't got a leg to stand on unless I lie."

"No, that's not you, lad, I know you'll take your medicine, however nasty it tastes. Still, that Ivy doesn't know anything for a fact and to try and ruin a man's career, it's a step too far Jarvis, it's downright devious if you ask me."

It was a low blow by anybody's standards I had to admit.

"She knew where to hit me where it hurt most. She always felt second fiddle to my work, so I hope she feels better for it."

"She's not the girl I thought she was," ma said, a note of disdain in her voice, "but I might have been misguided by her future prospects. You might just have had a lucky escape son."

There was no 'might' about it for me, a life with Ivy would have been a life of purgatory.

We sat with our shared thoughts a while and I could feel my eyes dropping from the warmth of the fire.

"What are you going to do about Pip?" ma asked eventually, making me sit up and take notice of the complex question.

My heart was heavy at the mention of her name. I have no idea what to do about Pip, and until all this blows over I can do nothing but wait.

"I'll have to bide my time, especially now Ferguson is dead."

Thoughts of Pip and Charlie back at the station answering questions about Ferguson's death ran through my mind and still haunt me now. They were taken into separate rooms and grilled for over an hour.

As Pip left the interview room, I came face to face with her and I had another feeling I'd never had before. I wanted to take her hand and leave the station; I wanted to go back to her little cottage and just sit and hold her hand by the fire, to allow her to feel how much she means to me in the quietness of that lovely room. I was overwhelmed by the thought of it. She looked like a little girl lost; her blue eyes reddened from weeping after the shock had worn off. I wanted to peel back the endless layers of pain in those eyes, to be rid of them for good.

Mr Douglas was going to see Pip home as Charlie was being remanded to the Bridewell in Leeds where he would be held for further questioning. It would then be for the magistrate to decide if he should be sent to the Assizes to stand trial and on what charge.

So much had changed since they'd arrived in Ackley only hours before. I watched them from the window until they disappeared from view, remembering why gentle, good-hearted Charlie had lost his reason. It could just as easily have been him lying on the slab and I still know without a doubt which one of the two men I would prefer to be left standing.

Then, alone in my room I sat down and wrote my statement with great care and attention to detail. I didn't want to risk missing out anything that happened in Ferguson's barn earlier in the day. After I'd finished, I stared at the words for the longest time knowing once my signature was on the bottom of the page there could be no going back.

My statement said Ferguson had attacked Charlie, who had no option but to defend himself. There would have to be a court case, but I hoped it would reduce the charge to manslaughter and any subsequent sentence. Charlie Metcalfe, in fear of his life had acted in self-defence.

Sighing, I put pen to paper and scrolled my signature across the page then blotted it before putting it into the new manilla folder with the name *Brendan Ferguson* written on the front in Rodge's handwriting.

For the second time in my career, I had compromised my position as a policeman.

And I would do it again tomorrow for the love of Miss Phillipa Metcalfe.

Chapter 24
1892 - Maureen

The shop bell is my summons to serve.

Day after day, barring Sundays, it tinkles away, sometimes seconds in between each ring, sometimes minutes but the sound of it is starting to slowly drive me mad. I have no life because of it. I might be elbow deep in soap suds but if that bell goes, what does it matter? It is my command to drop everything I'm doing and do someone else's bidding, and about ninety-five out of one hundred of those 'someone else's' aren't fit to shine my shoes.

There's the odd diamond, generally of the older generation, whose face lights up when they see me bob my head around the door to attend to their needs but the rest either want to moan, or gripe about my prices, or in the case of the worst ones, barely bother to look the side I'm on while I'm fetching and carrying for them. This didn't affect me quite so much once, I need their money above all else, but the last few years it's started to get under my skin. I don't know if it's that I've changed or if I've just seen the light and now I can't unsee it.

However, there is one customer who isn't old at all who I look forward to seeing, though I doubt she'll know it: Pip Metcalfe. She comes in every Saturday afternoon, all meek and timid but somehow, I can always tell she's listening to me. I like her quiet way and how she doesn't like to be the centre of attention. She's more like her father than her mother. I didn't much like Orla Metcalfe, but then I struggled to be civil to her after that day she blew my life up in my face. I know you shouldn't speak ill of the dead, but I would have been grateful for her keeping her trap shut and minding her own business.

It's odd because I don't associate Pip with her mother in my mind, which surprises me considering how I felt about her before she died. After her mother left them, I thought a lot about young Pip; how dignified she was, how she stepped up to the plate to look after her father and brother. One day, right out of the blue and for no particular reason, I found myself comparing her to Ivy.

Pip couldn't be any less like my daughter and the comparison of the two girls suddenly made me uncomfortable. My family are different, Ivy doesn't lift a finger and Walter, well he's either out, or if he isn't I'm wishing he was. Perhaps my grandmother would have said I'd made my own bed in being too accommodating and putting myself last all the time. Perhaps my grandmother would have been right, but then I wasn't top of her list either, so perhaps I just carried on where I left off with her.

I think it was about three years after Orla Metcalfe told me about Walter's 'indiscretions' when everything changed in our house. Three years is a long time, I'd left myself stewing too long for my own good. Then the stew boiled over and left a ruddy great mess I could never clean up properly.

Walter was coming and going as he pleased, sloping off to see Norma Granger every opportunity, blissfully unaware I'd been put in the picture by a relative stranger who I can only assume thought she was acting in my best interests.

We'd been in separate beds for about six years by then because I liked to turn in early due to my early morning deliveries and Walter staying out late. It was a 'before and after' situation. Before I discovered what was going on with Norma, I'd sleep right through, never even aware of him coming up to bed. I was tucked up snugly and slept like a top.

Then afterwards it was a different story; I'd wait for him to come home, that woman's scent choking me, and more because I realised it had been there all along. It was faint as he always made sure he had a swill in the bowl, but it was still there alright by morning, taunting me as a silly, old fool. Walter Davies had turned me into a laughingstock.

Then I'd lie there listening to him driving the pigs' home with his disgusting snoring until around two or three in the morning. I was up at five, so I faced the day ahead worn out before it had even started. Many a night I'd lie waiting, listening out, and think this is the night I'll tell him after I'd got myself all worked up. When I heard the door go, my heart would pound out of my chest, and I'd slide the words I'd rehearsed to the very tip of my tongue. I'd even draw breath to say them out loud, but then my mouth would clamp shut of its own accord, and I'd gulp the words back down and just pretend I was asleep. The only reason I didn't say them was very simple: I might have hated the sight of him, but I was terrified he would leave me. I was terrified I'd be left to fend for Ivy and myself with the meagre pot of money the shop gave us. It wouldn't have sat well with me, but more so it wouldn't have sat well with a daughter who had grown accustomed to a certain standard of living.

So, me and Walter were left tethered together.

Sundays were the worst. In the week, he left for work, came home, read the paper, then sloped off to the pub. Even during the short amount of time when he graced us with his presence I was in and out of the shop, so he wasn't under my feet.

But Sundays were different. The shop was closed as the day was a day of rest and time to spend with family, going to church, talking to each other. The pubs opening a couple of hours at lunchtime and not again until the early evening meant the men were there all day. I used to think of the Metcalfe's out in the sticks and envy them that they liked living in each other's pockets. Or at least it seemed that way … until I was enlightened.

I've no idea what he's like with Norma, but at home Walter's not a talkative man. The odd comment is all that ever passes his lips and usually those comments are dull as dishwater. For long enough I was just content he wasn't a cruel man as Sundays could be worse for some of the customers with their men. Boredom is one thing, fear and dread quite another.

Ivy spent many a long hour in her room until she started seeing Jack and then Jarvis. Her time before she started courting them was spent reading, preening, lounging because my daughter and I have one thing in common: we don't have any friends. This should have set the alarm bells ringing about the kind of girl Ivy had turned into, but I thought it was just because she was too good for the girls at school. At least I had my friends at school, until I gave them up for Walter.

I remember that particular Sunday vividly. Ivy was out for a walk with Jack, and I'd kept her tea warm in the range. I'd said we were eating as we always did at a quarter past two after chucking out time at the pub. Ivy knew this well enough, but she came and went as she pleased. I've noticed it now, but I didn't then as I had my head up my own backside in those days.

Walter came in the door, and I jumped up to dish out the scrag end of beef I'd had cooking since seven o'clock that morning so it was nice and tender, and a knife could slide through it like butter. I'm a good cook though I say it myself. I learnt from my grandmother as my mother died when I was ten. Gran made it plain that she was too old to look after a young girl, so she put me to good use. Cooking, sewing, knitting—she taught me them all and made sure I had plenty of practice.

That Sunday, Walter looked a bit worse for wear, but he never had more than two pints because he's a bit of a penny-pincher is Walter which is why I never have a lot of money for food. He liked to save his money for our old age he said, but by then I'd found out where it was really going. He kept smart, his grey balding hair thick and wavy except for small patch at the crown which he disguised well. His job at the mill meant he was quite slim without the paunch most middle-aged people seemed to develop, me included. We used to fancy each other in the early days, and I would still have fancied him if other emotions weren't at the forefront of my mind by then. He didn't fancy me. He hadn't fancied me since I lost my figure after having Ivy. I thought that's what happened when you became parents, you reached an understanding, and all that stuff and nonsense went on the back shelf. I didn't have anyone to confide in or tell me otherwise, so I just assumed it was the same for everybody.

After his dinner Walter swigged his tea down from his mug and I got up from the table to take our plates and start washing up. It had started raining I remember, and it was bashing the kitchen window. Sundays in bad weather are even worse, they make you feel like you're hemmed in with nowhere to go. I thought I might take the opportunity to start knitting a new cardigan for Ivy. I'd bought some nice lemon wool and it would go lovely with the green dress I'd made her.

Walter's voice drifted into my mind, as I was almost looking forward to the afternoon by the fireside. He'd soon fall asleep and then I could make a start on that cardy.

"Them carrots were a bit hard," he said.

I stopped scouring the pan and looked out at the pouring rain in the yard, piecing together his few words. It was a straightforward enough statement I suppose, "Them carrots were a bit hard."

Before I knew what was happening, I'd swung around from the sink with the pan in my hand, suds dripping onto the flags of the floor. The pan somehow began to rise in the air, and I looked at it, wondering how it had got there. I didn't have time to wonder long though because then the pan flew from the air to crash down. It crashed right into the back of Walter's neck. I think it would have been alright but for force with which it landed, making his head fall forward to land on the table, his hands falling by the sides of his thighs sitting on the chair.

He was clean out of it, looking as though he'd fallen asleep when Ivy suddenly appeared in the kitchen. I remember thinking she was making the floor all muddy and cluttering the place up with her soggy umbrella and gloves on the dresser top.

"He drunk?" she asked, part question, part statement.

Nodding, I put the pan back into the suds and started scrubbing like I could scrub it clean away forever.

"Ay, he's had one too many today for some reason I'll never find out. I'll get him up to bed in a minute if you go get some dry clothes on. Then you can have your dinner while I start knitting that new cardy for you I was telling you about."

"What new cardy?" she asked heading towards the stairs, taking off her hat as she went.

If I'd mentioned that cardy once, I'd mentioned it ten times and how I thought it would look nice, I'd even shown her the wool. I don't know why I was surprised she hadn't been listening.

Pip Metcalfe would be delighted to have a cardy her mother had knitted, I thought, before suddenly remembering Walter out cold on the kitchen table.

"Come on, old lad up with you," I said, putting his limp arm around my shoulder. It was handy I was twice the size of him, so it was quite easy to get him upstairs. I took his shoes off and put him fully clothed into bed, tucking the eiderdown right under his chin. Standing in the chilly bedroom I stared down at him for a while until I heard Ivy going downstairs. Walter looked so peaceful lying there and I tidied his hair with my fingers before heading down to dish up Ivy's dinner.

"I'm off up for a lie down too," she said after eating half of it, the rest she pushed to one side before setting her knife and fork down. No word of thanks, or by your leave if I recall.

Then I washed Ivy's plate up and fetched my knitting basket from under the stairs. I sat by the fire listening to the rain on the window in the cosy parlour, finally managing to make a start on that bloody cardy.

Chapter 25
1892 - Pip

Today is not Christmas Day. It may be to millions of others in the world, but not to us.

Everything is worse at Christmas, so they say, and they say it because it's true. The happiness of the season is snatched away and watching others celebrating seems cruel. Rightly or wrongly, that's exactly how it feels.

The last days have been dreadful. With my mother gone, we were going to try and make the best of it. But now there's another death hanging over us… and however much we might like to deny it, my father has blood on his hands.

Liam has arrived and brought the cold in with him. He hangs his outdoor things on the rack by the door then warms his hands over the fire.

"Hello, you two," he says, making his way over to plant a clumsy kiss on my cheek. He smells of smoke and beer but it's familiar and not unpleasant. Today I hold on to my brother a bit longer than usual when I hug him. Laughing awkwardly, he squirms away telling me he can't breathe. But I know he's embarrassed and I'm sorry I did it now. I should remember he's too old to be overly affectionate, but sometimes I can't help myself.

"The Morton's have sent some food. Nothing fancy, just a meat pie and fresh carrots from their garden. They know we've got plenty of potatoes."

Ordinarily this would make us laugh.

"Oh, and there's a fruit loaf too," he says, pulling everything out of the cloth bag that's seen better days. I'll have to make them a new one to say thank you.

"That's nice of them," my father and I say at the same time.

Ordinarily this would make us laugh too.

Liam looks at us and sighs, going over to sit on the settle near my father.

"Look, whichever way we look at it, today's going to be a long day and I think we should take the opportunity to have a proper chat about the future," he says.

My father taps his pipe on the fire grill and then stuffs it with tobacco before lighting it with a spill. I know he's considering Liam's words all the while he's doing it.

"Inspector Blackburn says you acted in self-defence da, and that will be taken into account," he says.

I can't look at him. I'll get used to it, but the lie sits heavily on my shoulders, sometimes making me short of breath like it's winded me. I'll have to get used to it. Ferguson killed my mother I know it, and it could just as easily have been my father who fell and banged his head in the scuffle.

I settle down in my chair to join the conversation. Liam's right, we must talk about things properly and prepare for any eventuality.

I decide to be brave and get the ball rolling, but my father beats me to it.

"There are things I must tell you," he says, "you're both adults now, and you deserve to know the truth. In fact, I've decided I owe you the truth on behalf of your mother."

How unprecedented; here was I expecting to plan a way forward for us, instead it seems skeletons are to be hauled from the closet.

Oh da, I think as his eyes fill with tears, you don't owe us anything, not a single brass tack. He draws on his pipe while we watch him intently.

"Well, I'm pointing out the obvious when I say your mother was different to most people; I know I don't need to tell you that, but I have to start somewhere. She was a deep-thinker and she'd learned a lot of hard lessons she felt it important to pass on, especially to you as her daughter, Pip."

I somehow manage a pensive smile of encouragement for my father who's clearly floundering. Liam and I are leant forward hanging on to his every word though we know already this will be no fairy tale with a happy ending.

"It will come as a side swipe to you, Liam I'm afraid, because I haven't mentioned it since Ferguson spilled the beans in front of Pip. When your mother ran away from Ireland, she *was* having a baby. Ferguson wasn't lying about that."

Liam looks quickly between us both, his face hanging loose with shock.

"I'm sorry, lad, I know you're playing catch-up with the story but that was the last thing Ferguson said before he died, so it floored our Pip as you can imagine. I didn't know how to bring it up and I wasn't sure until today if we should tell you, but secrets are what break people and families, and we shouldn't have them anymore."

Liam reaches for my hand, holding on to it tightly suddenly realising the full implication behind the confession. I'm not sure if I would ever have told him what Ferguson said if it was left up to me.

My father puts his pipe on the stand then leans towards us so we're sitting in a huddle.

"Don't fret, Pip, Brendan Ferguson isn't your father if that's what you've been thinking. He can't be your father because sadly, the baby didn't survive. The worry of fleeing her homeland and leaving her family behind was too much for your mother as you can only imagine. I'm sorry to tell you she lost the baby."

Liam drops my hand and lets out an enormous breath, sagging in his seat. The relief is clearly seeping out of him along with the air.

"Da, I'm sorry to hear we lost our brother or sister, truly I am, but … but I'm relieved that man isn't Pip's father," he spins his head my way, "I'm so glad, Pip for so many reasons."

I reach to pat his leg saying, "I know, Liam, I feel the same. I couldn't bear the thought that man was of my blood," I turn to my father, "but I need you to know it wouldn't have made a blind bit of difference to how I felt about you da, I hope you can believe me."

His eyes close, so the tear that was long-threatening to appear slips down his cheek and I jump up to slide my arms around his neck.

"I can love, I can," he whispers, "and I would have been the same."

The turmoil this man has lived through is beyond belief. Is it any wonder he was pushed to breaking point?

"You know, I've been thinking, there's at least one good thing to come out of this," Liam says, "mam didn't leave us of her own accord, he must have used the threat of being exposed as a bigamist to blackmail her into going to live there. It's obvious; did you think of that?"

"Not at first I didn't, I'll be honest," my father says, "I thought she was torn between me, and Ferguson and she wanted to stay near her children in the hope of you still seeing her. That was some of it I think, but I bet he enjoyed her being so near yet so far from you. It will have been part of her punishment for leaving him." He pauses to look at us both almost sheepishly, "Did you ever go see her?" he asks.

I stare at the floor then swallow, but it's no use, I can't swallow down the lie. I must bring him some comfort no matter what Liam's thoughts are on the matter.

"I did go see her a few times, yes. I even took her some shopping occasionally when I knew Ferguson would be out."

I can't bring myself to look at Liam, he'll resent me for this, perhaps never forgive me but I was caught between the devil and the deep blue sea.

"I did too," Liam confesses as we stare at him, "only once, and I couldn't do it again, but we left on good terms. I couldn't go back because it was too much for me to handle. I wish I had now of course, but by the end of the night I think we'd reached an understanding."

My, this is a night for an array of family secrets to be disclosed it seems.

"I'm pleased you went, Liam, for mam and for you. At least you don't have to wrestle with any more demons than you do already."

"It can't have been easy, but it will have meant the world to her," my father says, running his white handkerchief over each cheek in turn. By the time he's finished, he looks more like my old da.

Standing up I look down on my family, feeling wrung out like a wet rag by our talk. It must have been incredibly difficult for my father to broach the sensitive subject, but I'm proud of him that he found the courage from somewhere.

"I think I'll warm that pie, what do you say? Who needs goose when we've been sent a pie made with love?"

They each hand me a weak smile. I pat my father's hand then head to put the pie gifted to us by Liam's future in-laws in the range. He needs to marry Sarah after the trial. It's time, and if the worst happens heaven forbid, he can move in here with his bride. We'll all rub along just fine I'll make sure of it.

Something moving catches my eye through the window.

What's that I wonder? I push my face closer to the glass and rub a hole in the steam with a tea towel.

Perhaps it might be better to ask *who* is that?

It looks as though we're having visitors this Christmas Day … whether we like it or not.

Chapter 26
1892 - Jarvis

"Ma, what the heck are you doing here?"

Her face is all red and glowing with perspiration. She's been running; I don't remember seeing my mother run an inch in her life.

"Sit down," I say pulling out a chair on the other side of the table. She plonks herself down unceremoniously, fighting to get her breath. I rub her back to try and calm her down. I'd like to know why she's come to the pub to fetch me on Christmas Day when in less than an hour's time I'd be home eating my dinner with her. I hand her my beer, and she takes a long glug where she'd normally take a ladylike sip. That is if I could get her to hold a pint glass in her hand in the first place. "Ladies do not drink pints," I can hear her saying.

"Jarvis," she says in a low voice, "get your things, get a horse from a stable, quick," she says taking three great gulps of air while I look on alarmed, "Maureen and Ivy are on their way to see Pip Metcalfe. I saw them set off on Walter's cart and I've had to run here to fetch you. You'll have to get up there straightaway, never mind your beer. I think it should be you who goes to sort it out under the circumstances.

Pip and Ivy in the same sentence can only mean one thing: trouble is afoot, and I must be on my way.

"Come on," I say, "tell me what you know while I ask Ken Morton if I can borrow his horse."

Ma jumps up from her seat to stand with me while I throw my overcoat on.

"How did you come to see them?" I ask her.

She looks coy as she scurries by my side, trying to keep up.

"Well, I was getting the dinner ready and ... and I might have had one or two sherries and I might have been on my way to the shop to give Ivy Davies a piece of my mind."

"You were doing what?" I ask, still rushing out the back door of the pub to head to Ken Morton's house, "What the hell were you going to do that for?"

She chooses to ignore my bad language, saying, "Jarvis, I'm sorry believe me, and I don't know if I'd have gone through with it, but when I got near the shop, I saw them heading away on the cart and then turn off towards Metcalfe's cottage. That's the only place they could be heading. Nobody goes up that way if they can help it."

I think briefly of my days spent at that cottage and close my eyes to Pip's face. I picture that face too many times nowadays. Thank God Charlie's home. I must make haste as these things can get out of hand, as I know only too well from recent experience. Here was I, expecting a dull Christmas Day.

It only takes a minute for Ken to come to the door and for me to explain I need to borrow his horse if he would be so kind, but not his cart. I try to keep the urgency from my voice.

Ma is holding onto my arm, still catching her breath.

"Of course, inspector, come with me," he says, making me wonder briefly what he knows. The public story is that I'm taking a break due to exhaustion from the case, but Ivy might have set the record straight with whoever would listen in the village by now.

We head over the road to the old barns where a few people keep their horses, including Walter Davies. Ken saddles his chestnut horse with the hands of a man who does it often, saying, "You alright Mrs B, sit on the stool there afore you fall down."

Ma sits down gladly, leaning forward to place her hands on her knees.

"Where you headed?" Ken asks me.

"I just need to pay a visit to the Metcalfe's with some news. Sergeant Rogerson has taken King out and I've no idea when he'll be back," I lie.

Ken knows better than to ask what the news is thankfully, so I'm off the hook.

"Well, I shan't be needing her all day, so no rush to get back," he says as I mount.

Ma walks at the side of me back to the road, then I thank Ken for his trouble as he heads back home to his family.

"I'm sorry, Jarvis, I don't know what I was thinking interfering like that with Ivy," she says quietly.

"I know, but in a strange way it's a good job you did," I say, "just go back home and I'll see you there in a while when I know what's going on at *Sunnyside*."

She walks backwards in the opposite direction towards home, saying loudly over the clip clopping of Ken's horse, "Heaven knows what's got into them both."

I've no time to discuss it but I know what's got into them both: a dose of the green-eyed monster. To go out there today of all days though when they should be enjoying a day at home having a nice Christmas dinner, it doesn't seem right.

I can't help recalling the last time I was sitting astride a horse. My conscience swells like it does every time I think of that day. But it's too late dwelling on it now, I've done what I've done so that's that and I'll have to live with it like everything else.

Ken's horse is young and lithe, so we pound across the moors at a gallop. She's sure-footed, so it cuts so much off the journey when I don't need to stick to a footpath. Jumping the hedges and tufts of heather, it's like they're not even there. It's a good job as Maureen and Ivy had a decent head start on me.

The cottage finally comes into view and Walter's horse and cart is waiting outside the wide-open door. Abandoning Ken's horse by the side of it I race inside to face my fate.

"Now, I've told you, Mrs Davies," Charlie is saying, "don't come to my house causing bother. If you want to speak civilly, then we're all ears, but I'd thank you to keep your name-calling to yourself."

As I enter the kitchen, every face turns my way. Maureen and Ivy are wearing their coats and hats, standing by the window and Pip, Charlie and Liam have their back to the fire. The settle stands between them, and there's barely room for one more inside.

"Oh, here he is, the man of the hour," Maureen says sarcastically, turning her nose up like I'm a bad smell that's wafted in from outside. Ivy's expression is a mirror image. "What brings you here today I wonder?"

"Mrs Davies, Ivy, this is neither the time nor the place for this discussion," I say, whipping my hat off with force of habit, "you've obviously come looking for trouble and this family have enough to worry about at present, don't you think? Please, come back to our house and speak with me there if you would."

Ivy rolls her eyes, but it's Maureen who speaks first.

"Enough to worry about; I'm sick of hearing about this bloody family. To think, I felt sorry for that young lass being abandoned by her mother and it turns out she's no better than she is … was. She stole you away from our Ivy when her back was turned and I'm not having it, I'm not standing for it!"

Maureen takes a step in Pip's direction, and I rush to stop her going any further. Holding onto her arm I try to steer her outside, but Ivy bats my hand away from her mother.

"Get off her," she says, her tone menacing, but far calmer than her mother's. I'm not sure which is more unnerving.

Pip looks horrified by the scene and I'm all too aware that it's me who's responsible for bringing this trouble to her door. If I could only get Maureen and Ivy outside, it would certainly help matters. This tiny room is closing in on us.

"Please, just come with me and I'll explain everything. Don't blame Pip, it's not her fault. I'm not here as a policeman and I'd like to pay you the respect of telling you the whole story if you'll let me."

They may be glowering but they're quiet for now at least. I might just have managed to make them see reason.

Ivy huffs and barges past me on her way out the door. Maureen follows suit like an obedient dog, and I watch the back of them disappear with a sense of relief.

"I'm sorry, really I am," I say to Pip, but directing it to the whole family, "I'll come back, and we'll talk, but for now we need to get out of here so I can sort this sorry situation out once and for all."

The paleness of Pip's face is upsetting me, preventing me from leaving as swiftly I should.

"Until later then, Inspector Blackburn," Charlie says, nodding towards the door. I feel dismissed.

I set off to join the women to accompany them back to Ackley. I must ensure I stay by their side all the way because I can't risk them working each other up to lead them back here again.

"Jarvis," Charlie says as I head off. I turn around, surprised he's used my name. "Make sure you do come back, lad, there's a lot to discuss."

I glance once more at Pip whose eyes have followed me all the way to the door.

Nodding, I've no idea what her father means by that statement. I'm only glad he'll let me back in the house again.

I'll just have to try and put the Metcalfe's to the back of my mind for the first time in a while.

I've got a long, uncomfortable ride home ahead of me.

Chapter 27
1892 - Jarvis

I took Ken's horse back and he wished me a merry Christmas as I left the barn trying my best not to run. It sounded odd hearing the usual greeting but even odder saying it back.

It was a quiet return journey to the village with Maureen and Ivy licking their wounds and pretending I wasn't riding at the side of their cart. I asked them to meet me at our house in a quarter of an hour's time so I could return Ken's horse, and here they are right on cue I see.

"I'm back, ma, we've got company," I call as I go inside.

Ma appears in the passageway, looking over my shoulder to see a po-faced Ivy and her mother. Her face is free of expression, and she doesn't comment.

"Come on in," I say as ma sets off for the best room.

I watch her walking up the passageway and briefly notice her back is slightly bent. When did my ma get a stoop? I have a sudden pang of guilt that I hadn't noticed it before now. Another wave comes when I think about her being worried sick about me, not just today, but all the days I used to go to work before I was suspended. She will have felt the same way with dad too, so no wonder her shoulders are buckling under the strain, she's had a lifetime of worry piled on them.

"I'll take your coats," I say to Maureen and Ivy holding out my hand.

Maureen steps away like I've spat at her saying, "No, thank you all the same, we'll not be stopping."

I shrug and take off my own coat before stepping into my house shoes.

Joining ma in the best room I think it's apt we should be sitting in here as this room is only used on Christmas Days. She points to the settee opposite the fireplace then Maureen and Ivy perch on the edge with their handbags on their laps. Me and ma sit in the two chairs as I smell the stuffed turkey crown cooking on the range since early morning no doubt. It smells like Christmas it looks like Christmas, yet I wonder if it will ever feel the Christmas spirit again after today.

Me and ma exchange a glance, but I know the first move is mine alone to make.

"Thanks for coming here," I say, "it's all been very upsetting, and it's time for me to explain myself."

I must choose my words carefully and not risk making a bad situation worse. It might surprise them that I'm prepared to take full responsibility for what's happened. I never wanted to let Ivy down.

"I didn't expect to be snowed in at the cottage that week of course, it wasn't planned. I had plenty of time to think which I didn't like at first but then I eventually took the opportunity."

Ivy sniffs and laughs but not kindly.

"Yes, we know you took the opportunity alright. I was forgotten about quicker than two shakes of a lamb's tail. One week, one rotten week was all it took," she says.

"Ivy, I told you not long ago, we just aren't right for each other. We want different things and …"

"Look, you've got to see it from our side, Jarvis," Maureen talks loudly over me, "all I ever wanted was for our Ivy to find a good lad to settle down with and you were him. You seemed keen enough, so you've led her on is my way of thinking."

"Now hang on a minute, Mrs Davies," ma says, sliding forward in her seat "my boy did nothing of the sort. He's not some Jack the Lad type character who plays fast and loose with a girl's feelings."

Maureen and Ivy's cheeks are glowing, and I doubt it's just because they're angry. They must be overheating in their coats and hats now the room is heating up.

"And I'm disappointed in you, Ivy, going to the police station to report our Jarvis. That was sneaky and mean," ma says.

Both the other women shoot their eyes towards her.

"Sneaky and mean," Maureen hisses, "it's your son who's been sneaky, and with that Metcalfe girl of all people. Filthy little dog she is, like her mother."

Heat rushes up my chest and I grip the chair arms.

"Look you two, I'm sick of you slating Pip Metcalfe when she's done nothing wrong, I'm the one to blame here. Her mother hasn't been in the grave two minutes, and you still can't help yourself spouting

186

nastiness about her. You're all the same in this damn village."

Maureen jumps up, and ma and Ivy join her, but I stay seated as I'm fast losing my temper.

"Don't you swear at me Jarvis Blackburn, I'm sick of you defending Orla Metcalfe and her family. That bloody woman ruined my life and our Ivy's life. I hate her with every breath in my body, and I'll hate her to my dying day. Everything unravelled after she came and told me about Walter's fancy woman, everything. All our lives ruined because Orla Metcalfe couldn't keep her trap shut. I'm bloody well glad somebody smothered the living daylights out of her and now she's lying cold in that grave. I'll be dancing on it soon enough."

The outburst hangs in the air all around us, the words floating around our heads like debris from a demolished building.

I look at Maureen, her face distorted in anger until I barely recognise her as the woman from the corner shop that I've known all my life.

The meaning of her words sink in slowly, like a photographic image developing in fluid. Mrs Turton from next door hammers on the wall, her muffled shout telling us to keep the noise down.

Finally, I find my voice.

"What makes you think Orla Metcalfe was smothered to death, Mrs Davies?" I ask her quietly and as innocently as I can muster, the detective returning to the case.

Maureen's expression gives away she's suddenly become aware of the significance of her outburst too.

She looks away from me then sits back down on the settee like somebody's pushed her with some force. She coughs a couple of times into her clenched palm to delay matters. I've seen it all before.

"Well, everybody knows how she died, don't they? I mean it's common knowledge as far as I'm aware. What're you getting at? You better be careful what you're saying lad, very careful indeed."

I sit down as do ma and Ivy, their eyes upon me.

"I didn't know it was common knowledge because it shouldn't have been," I say calmly.

She lifts her shoulders saying, "Well, you know how people talk around here. There are no secrets in Ackley, Jarvis, you know that as well as anyone."

There is desperation in every word.

"Yes, you're right but most of the rumours I've heard around and about are that she was strangled."

Ma nods as if to corroborate my statement.

"And I can tell you we were happy to let that go. We have yet to establish who killed Orla Metcalfe and have deliberately not revealed the coroner's report into the cause of death."

My mind is working overtime, pulling all the pieces together.

The fire swiftly goes out of Maureen's eyes, and she's suddenly lost for words when she had so much to say for herself only seconds ago. We all sit watching her now in silence as she searches frantically for the right thing to say next.

But it's not long before she realises that she's said far too much already for me to just brush it all under the carpet.

In a few short minutes, Maureen Davies from the corner shop will be accompanying me to the police station to answer more questions, Christmas Day or not.

Suspended from duty or not.

Chapter 28
1892 - Pip

He was true to his word and I'm secretly delighted.

Jarvis has just arrived to have that long overdue discussion. I've taken his coat and he's settling himself by the fire and all the while we haven't taken our eyes off each other. I know I should be nervous but it's just like he's come back home to me.

Liam left first thing to spend Boxing Day with Sarah's family like he's done for the last two Christmases. Normally my father and I would spend the day together playing cards and draughts, but we decided not to put ourselves through it and have business as usual. Now I couldn't be happier with that decision.

Jarvis doesn't ask to see my father and I don't offer to get him from his workshop. This is our moment … just for us. We've both been pining for it.

"I'll tell you what happened yesterday when your da comes in for dinner, but I'd like to talk to you first," he says, "will you sit down with me awhile?"

I stare at him a moment thinking how much I've missed his face, the way his brown eyes are wide open when he talks to me like he has nothing to hide.

"Well, if I must," I say smiling.

Truly I can't think of anything I'd like to do more. As we sit side by side on the tiny settle Liam and

I used to share growing up, the comfort of familiarity is just the same. Peace is in my heart for the first time in years, and even if it only turns out to be for today, I will be grateful for it.

He slides his fingers into mine and our hands lay entwined on my lap, nestled in the folds of my skirts. We look at them, both of us enjoying the wonderful newness of the experience.

"The time we had together was so bitter-sweet Pip," he says his voice almost a whisper, "but one day you will be completely happy. It will take time and patience to mend the wounds, but I vow this day to be the one to make you happy."

I'm unable to respond as my throat is in a tangled mess. This man is mine and that alone will mend me in time, I think. Leaning my head on his shoulder I let the calmness wash over me like a warm breeze.

It doesn't last long enough.

"What about your job?" I ask eventually, "What will happen if they decide to sack you? I can't live with the thought of it when I know it's because of your feelings for me."

His thumb is gently caressing the back of my hand, but he doesn't jump to waylay my concerns as I expected. Instead, he asks me a question: "Have you ever had time to just stop and think?

I don't need to think about it long.

"Well yes, I suppose I have," I say unsure what he's getting at.

He sighs, my head following the rise and fall of his shoulders.

"Well, now I have. It might not have been in quite the way I wanted but I've come to see it as a blessing in disguise."

Lifting my head I stare at his profile, the strong straight nose, the eyelashes longer than my own, his powerful neck muscles. I've never had the opportunity to study his face in detail before, our kisses were in the darkness of the night.

He turns his face my way, his sparkling eyes telling me what he has discovered during recent times is profound. I understand because I have made the very same discovery. But this still doesn't answer my question.

"Like most sons, when I was a boy, I wanted to be my dad. He came home in his uniform, and I used to feel like nothing could ever hurt us when he was around. He showed me how to polish boots so you could see your face in them, shine buttons to a blinding gleam, all the things you'd expect from a father who was a policeman. Like Liam, I wanted to follow my dad, I wanted to be him. But I never stopped to think for a minute if I really *wanted* to do what he did—I was going to be policeman when I grew up and I never questioned that fact, not once."

His eyes have strayed to the fire, his mind taking him far back in time.

"I expect I'll get a rap on the knuckles, perhaps a warning for being involved with you during the … the case, but I'd be able to pick up where I left off and carry on. I've never put a foot wrong, and we were in extreme circumstances so it will all blow over in time,

I'm sure of it. I could tread water whilst I waited for it to blow over of course.

I could, except I've realised being a policeman isn't what I want to do for the rest of my working life."

What can he mean? He hasn't given it enough thought surely, he's just lost his way because he's been suspended that's all it is. I sit forward on the settle turning my whole body towards him to make sure he knows he has my full attention.

"Jarvis, please listen carefully. You've had a knockback but you're one step away from being a chief inspector like your dad. You might have to wait a bit longer because of blotting your copy book, but in a few years, you'll achieve your dream. Don't give up on it now and don't give up on it because of me because you'll grow to hate me. Perhaps not at first, but eventually you will think of me as the one who stood in the way of you becoming what you always wanted to be in life."

I'm startled when he reaches to quickly grasp both my hands in his.

"Pip, I've realised now the dream was never mine. I was following my dad's footsteps without giving any thought to it being the path I wanted to tread. It was dad's dream, not mine, I only carried it on for him, not for me. I know it wholeheartedly now I've been handed the gift of time to discover it for myself."

I'm not convinced. A person doesn't doggedly chase something all their adult life only to suddenly turn their back on it. He's deluded.

Both his palms now come up to cover my cheeks, and he stares into my eyes, searching far deeper than anyone ever before.

"I had nothing else but that goal to focus on. I was paying lip service to it and there was nothing to show me I never even wanted it in the first place. Believe me my love when I tell you I've never been more certain of anything before. Even if you decided you didn't want me, I still wouldn't want to carry along the same road I've been on. The two are entirely different things that just so happen to be joined."

He leans to touch my lips with his own and I close my eyes, taken unawares by the pleasure it gives me in a place I've never thought about before in such a way. The longing for this man is taking my breath away.

"Oh Pip, my sweet girl," he whispers between kisses, "I was sent here to save you, I came here to be saved by you. All our lives we have served others in our own different way; now I want to devote myself to serving you, I'd like to give you a life no less than you deserve. I love you; I've loved you since I peered through the snow outside into the kitchen the very first day I came here, I just didn't know. I didn't know what love felt like then."

His words burrow inside my heart, and I want to lock them away so I might bring them out at will for tonight, tomorrow, whenever I don't quite believe he said them.

"I love you too, Jarvis," I say unabashed, "I'd like to recreate the time we spent together in this cottage, content just to sit with each other, be with each other. I know we could be happy in our little world out here."

My words are not as flowery as his, but they are true, and they are heartfelt. I know he believes me because I know him already and this wasn't something I had to force; it was the most natural thing in the world. Just like my mother and father we joined hearts without knowing and now I'm only glad we came together against all the odds. He is the silver lining in the dark cloud that's been following me around for so long.

I waited for him, and he found me.

Now, I believe what he was trying to make me understand because his decision is not about me. I've been lucky, I've always had plenty of time to think, to know what I want and don't want. Living out here gives you both and it's why I love it as I do. Once you have time, space in your head, perhaps then, and only then can you begin to know yourself truly.

"What will you do instead?" I ask, our faces almost touching still.

"I have some thoughts, many of them in fact. However, this is for another time. Right now, we must get your da because I have news. News which I think will come as a relief, yet beggar belief for the two of you."

What went on in the village yesterday after he left, I wonder. I've thought of nothing else since, until now.

"I took Maureen Davies down to the station for questioning yesterday," he says.

I pull my hand away, bemused suddenly at the change in direction of the conversation. Maureen Davies taken down to the station, what on earth has she got to do with anything?

"I thought we had Maureen bang to rights, case solved," he says, pulling me from my seat, "I had my eyes opened and thought I knew what I was looking at but oh, how wrong I turned out to be.

Come on, let's go get your da so I can explain everything."

Chapter 29
1892 - Jarvis

I would never have connected the dots because the dots were buried under a pile of lies and if you can't see all the dots, it's impossible to connect them.

I would have preferred to be the one asking the questions, but it was Mr Douglas who interviewed Maureen Davies on Christmas Day 1892.

In the end some good came out of bad, because if Maureen hadn't been consumed with jealously and resentment enough to confront Pip, then I might never have discovered her history with her mother.

Maureen didn't want any trouble, she didn't want the shame of being hauled away for questioning by the police in front of the neighbours, so I travelled with her to the station on Walter's horse and cart. I wasn't in my uniform so nobody would have been any the wiser if they happened to look out and spot us.

Ivy went home at her mother's insistence.

"When will you be back?" she asked, suddenly looking a little less certain of herself.

Maureen turned to me, but I couldn't shed any light. It would take as long as necessary and that was out of my hands.

Ivy sloped off down the ginnel, Maureen's face looking after her pinched with concern for her only child. Her father wasn't home but when he returned, she would have the job of explaining where her mother was. Maureen insisted she didn't want Walter to accompany us, and that at least wasn't a surprise.

What a dark horse her husband is. On the quiet journey to the station, I thought back to when I first discovered Walter and Norma Granger were having an affair. It was about nine years ago when ma told me and apparently, she was one of the last to know so it must have been even longer. All I remember thinking back then was that I didn't know Walter had it in him. He's not a bad looking bloke even now, but he's lacking a personality of any kind, good, bad, or indifferent, as non-descript as a chump of wood. Whereas Norma at the time was the most beautiful woman I'd ever set eyes on.

By the time we arrived at the station the last embers of the fire in Maureen had been snuffed out, so she was compliant. She shuffled ahead of me inside the building, restored to being the person I thought I knew so well.

A new face who I assumed was on loan from Leeds station was covering the front desk. Rodge will have been at home enjoying his dinner, ruddy-faced and happy after the extra pint at his local. He's such a creature of habit.

"Merry Christmas," the constable said, finishing off what he was writing.

"I'm Inspector Blackburn and this is Mrs Maureen Davies. May I ask your name?"

A pair of wide eyes preceded a startled face saying, "How do you do, inspector, I'm Constable Leighton. How may I help you today?"

"Might I see the officer in charge please?"

The constable jumped to his feet and nodded, telling me he would be back in a jiffy. The poor man will have had no idea if I could be allowed on the premises, so off he hurried to leave that decision to his superior officer.

Maureen had yet to utter a word since we left Ackley. Looking out of place in her best woollen coat and hat, she wasn't the type of clientele we were used to frequenting the station, not fitting into any of the usual categories.

Ever the professional, Mr Douglas's face was expressionless when we spoke. The conversation lasted over half an hour and during that time I was unable to tell if he was surprised by my revelation, irritated by the interruption to his day or anything else for that matter.

Then he disappeared into the interview room with Maureen and the constable. Before he left, he told me I would need to make a statement and, in the meantime to wait on one of the chairs in the foyer. I remember thinking I could have been getting a head start on my statement, but the station is no longer my home from home.

I did as I was told and waited a full five minutes, pacing the floor, staring at the clock on the wall behind the front desk. The hands of the clock were stuck surely, I thought.

Then I could stand it no longer, curiosity just got the better of me.

I knew if I sat outside the interview room, I'd be able to listen to what Maureen was saying. This was personal and I needed to know what had happened straight from the horse's mouth. Otherwise, I might never find out the full story and at that moment it was simply a thought I couldn't tolerate. I saw this as a sign of how much I'd changed or seen the light, whichever way I looked at it. Once upon a time I would never have disrespected rank and authority under any circumstances.

Placing a chair to wedge the foyer door open so I could make a speedy exit, if necessary, I pulled another chair from the desk nearest the interview room to settle down and listen to Maureen's story. I needed to get myself up to speed after the five-minute delay.

"There's no point backtracking, Mrs Davies, you've already said too much," Mr Douglas was saying to Maureen, "now, it's in your own best interests to cooperate."

"He's got it in for me has Jarvis Blackburn," she said, "he's mad at our Ivy for dobbing him in over that Metcalfe lass and he's just trying to get back at us."

"As I understand it you made your way to the Metcalfe's cottage earlier. I take it you weren't paying them a festive social call. I also understand that you stated in Inspector Blackburn's front room that Mrs Metcalfe had been smothered to death. May I remind you there were three witnesses to this. This information had not been released to the public. This is not looking good at all for you, I'm afraid."

There was a long pause. I could imagine Maureen weighing up her options, so she didn't play right into their hands.

"Please Mrs Davies, for the sake of your daughter, just tell us what you know."

There was yet more silence which went on for over two minutes, I know because I timed it.

Then suddenly a loud sigh bounced off the walls of the interview room startling me.

"Very well," she said, Maureen's tone then much less indignant."

I thought for a minute I'd misheard, pushing my head closer to the door to try and hear better what was being said.

"Good," Mr Douglas said levelly. I could imagine him sitting up a little straighter and checking Constable Leighton was doing due diligence with his note taking. Nothing could be missed, not one single word in these circumstances.

"These secrets are fair choking me. I may as well get them all off my chest because I'm only living half a life anyway. I should have controlled my temper today but it's too late for that so, now I suppose it's time to stand up and be counted. Anyway, life will never go back to being the same whichever way I play it."

I pictured the constable scribbling furiously, perhaps like me, never having taken down a true account of a confession to a murder before.

"Go on," Mr Douglas said, "though I wouldn't 'play' it at all if I were you."

"Alright then, but I think it will make more sense if I tell you the full story.

It's definitely no secret in the village that me and Walter have had our troubles. He made me into laughingstock because of his affair with Norma Granger but there was a time when I was living in blissful ignorance ..." she pauses.

"... that was until that Orla Metcalfe upset my applecart."

The first invisible dot had appeared when Maureen told me about Orla disclosing Walter's affair to her. Did Orla tell her with the best of intentions or otherwise, I wondered. Either way, I will never find out the answer; Orla has taken this to the grave with her.

"That woman took it upon herself to stick her nose in where it didn't belong," Maureen said, her pitch slightly raised by then, "she was doing it for me, she said, so Walter wasn't making a fool out of me, she said. Why couldn't she have just minded her own business? After she stuck her oar in, I had to face it all. I had to look at Walter every day knowing what he'd done, what he's still doing with another bloody woman.

Every damn thing changed that day. She toddled off after she dropped that little bombshell and left me to pick up the pieces. At first, I decided not to confront Walter, but then after about three years I think it was, it all came to a head ... literally. It was always going to happen one day."

Maureen let out a sinister little laugh that made the hairs on my neck stand up.

"I might as well tell you, I thought I'd killed him. I banged him over the head with a pan and he didn't wake up for three hours while I sat and knitted. Then he wandered downstairs in a stupor and all I could think was at least I won't hang. It should have filled me with relief, yet it didn't. I still had a life sentence living with a lying, cheating, selfish bugger of a husband.

I kept quiet about it and Walter thought he'd just got the mother of all hangovers. I tried to carry on for a few weeks, only glad I hadn't killed him. Then one Monday morning, I picked Walter's weekend shirt from the wash basket and dropped it. There was a small red stain on the collar. Not blood or anything dramatic like that, it was just a smudge of rouge or something, I think. I picked the shirt back up and held it at a distance like it was sullied or had a bad smell.

It was then I realised the shirt was exactly that. Every week I scrubbed and starched his shirts knowing they smelled of another woman, perhaps even had always had rouge stains on them from another woman. I just pretended not to notice.

Then without another thought, I screwed the shirt up in a tight ball and stuffed it in my basket by the door. I marched the six streets between us and knocked on the door of No. 6 Grove Road and knocked the door a little harder than intended. It drew a bit of attention and that was the one thing I've always hated, people knowing my business.

Norma Granger came to the door all rouged and bonny and I barged past her into her passageway. By the time I'd turned around she was hurrying to close the door behind me. The look on her face, it was worth doing it just for that.

I knew her Joe would be at work but to be honest I don't think I'd thought about it when I set off.

Pulling the dirty shirt out of my basket, I chucked it at her so it ruffled her perfect fair hair, and her mouth grew so wide a train could have gone through it.

"Norma," I said, "if you don't stop seeing my Walter this very day, I'll be telling your Joe. I hope you don't think I'm bluffing because you will be sorry if you call my bluff. I've put up with this situation for too long and now, woman to woman I'm telling you to call it off!"

She had the shirt in her hand, and she looked down at it and back again at me.

"I'm sorry, Maureen," she said, ready to go on but I shook my head.

"Shut up, I don't want to hear it! I just want you to hold up your end of the bargain so we can all move forward on a proper footing. It's not right and you know it. Now, if you do stop seeing him, and mind I'll know if you don't, then your Joe will be none the wiser, and you will be able to keep your family together. I'm sure your boys won't want their parents to split up but more, I don't think you'd want your husband to grow to hate you. I've seen the way he looks at you, I think you'd be stupid to spoil that love and that trust."

"How did you find out?" she asked.

I pulled my shoulders back and sniffed telling her Orla Metcalfe had been only too pleased to fill me in about what had been going on for years.

She looked shocked as well she might, then she started crying. I didn't care, I just skirted past her and let myself out of the front door. I wasn't interested in watching her pity tears.

"Everybody hated Orla Metcalfe and I can't imagine Norma felt any differently towards her. There was a whole village lined up waiting to lynch that woman for what she did to her family."

Maureen stopped talking. I waited to see who would have the next word.

"And did Mrs Granger stop seeing your husband?" Mr Douglas said after a moment of quiet.

"Oh ay, she did. I don't know if I would have told her Joe, but I didn't need to as it happens. The only thing was though, and this has been a bitter pill to swallow, Norma Granger wasn't, isn't my husband's fancy piece …. it was more than that I found out. It pains me to say that Walter's been pining for Norma ever since, even our Ivy's noticed which is a miracle in itself. The weights dropped off him and he's not sleeping and …"

I heard a sob from Maureen and for the first time I felt sorry for her. I shouldn't have, but I couldn't help it. I remembered calling in for a cuppa and sometimes an enlightening chat in the back room of the shop, particularly when I was a fresh-faced bobby. She was good to me.

"I see," Mr Douglas said, "so you blamed Mrs Metcalfe for all this, for ruining your life, not your husband and his mistress, I take it."

The sarcasm in his words didn't go unnoticed by me or by Maureen.

"You've no idea what it's been like," she spat, "it's been hell in our house, yet I've had to pretend we're playing happy families. I blamed him, he blamed me, it was a bloody nightmare I can tell you!"

"So, you decided to get your own back on Orla Metcalfe for ruining your life."

The silence went on and on then. I thought of them staring across at each other, eyes locked like horns and brimming with no end of emotions.

But no-one could have foreseen what came next.

"If I was you, I'd climb down from that high horse of yours right now, Chief Inspector. I wasn't the one who murdered an innocent woman, though I thought about it too many times believe me. I've got a temper yes, but I'm no cold-blooded killer."

Oh no, after all that it's not over yet then, I thought, my stomach flipping. Without her confession we were back to square one. My mind went straight to Pip, to Charlie, Liam and I felt sickened with disappointment. Justice for the family was as far away as ever.

"No, the deed wasn't done by my hand, it was done by my husband's, none other than Mr John Walter Davies. All those months he went without seeing Norma meant he had plenty of time to dwell on who had brought it all to a screeching stop for him and his ladylove. I was hoping to keep my family intact after he told me what he'd done one night when he'd had too much beer. Crying and wailing he was about how she'd brought it on herself, and he couldn't be blamed.

But now, as you think it was me who murdered Orla Metcalfe, I'm sure you understand that hell will freeze over before I swing from the noose for that man.

After all, I've got my Ivy to think of."

Chapter 30
1893 - Pip

I've lived a lifetime over the last year. So much pain, so much misery, but so much happiness and all in the name of love. My mother's love for us and for da; Jarvis's love for me; my love for him ... but there's one love that knocked me off my feet:

Walter Davies's love for Norma Granger.

He loved her. It wasn't just a fling or a bit of fun for years as everyone thought, it was true love. True love drove Walter Davies to ... to kill my mother in a crime of passion after he lost the love of his life.

Oh, the shock. It was the shock that prevented me feeling angry towards him for long enough. Anger towards a relative stranger is a peculiar thing I've found, because you don't know them, you can only imagine them as people. How they think, how they work is out of reach, so I've been left only guessing. Yesterday though I realised the anger has been steadily subsiding to be replaced by a relief that we finally know the truth when we might never have done. Nothing can bring my mother back, but we know why and how she was taken from us. I refuse to let my resentment towards that man ruin the rest of my life, I just can't let that happen.

There's something else too that I've been battling with. Why did my mother tell Maureen Davies about the affair after all she'd done herself? She was the one who always said that people in glass houses should never throw stones when people tittle-tattled, so it doesn't add up. At the time I suppose her secret was safe enough, but I've been trying and failing to understand why she felt she should interfere. It was clearly important to her yet whichever way I look at it I just don't think it was her place.

But regardless, she didn't deserve to lose her life over it. I realised recently that I can't keep churning a question I will never know the answer to over and over or I'll go mad. So, the last month I've been making a conscious effort to let go.

Liam is another story. He's not quite in the same place but I think I finally hit a nerve when I said he might lose Sarah if he didn't work out how to get past his anger. We can understand it, we can forgive him, but it's not fair on her and I told him so. I think he listened to me, so it's a start at least.

Liam's frustration has nowhere to go because Walter wriggled off the hook the end. The one thing that stopped him from hanging or even prosecution, was that a wife cannot testify against her husband and his wife's testimony was the only evidence. Did Maureen Davies know this when she spilled the beans at the station on Christmas Day? Somehow, I doubt it.

Perhaps Walter will spend the rest of his life wondering if other evidence will come to light, but for however long it lasts he can live with Norma and her two boys wherever they may be. They've gone and nobody knows where and I think that's for the best. Norma's husband is bereft as it turns out he was the only one who was in the dark about the affair. Fancy an entire village managing to keep a secret like that from you for a decade. I think about him often of late, how he had a wife and family and now he has nothing, not even a memory of their love because it's been spoiled.

Last July Ivy married Jack and he's moved into the shop. It may or may not be true love, but at least his money will save Maureen and Ivy losing their home along with their income. I haven't seen them since last Christmas Day when they descended on the cottage. I have to travel to the next village for my provisions nowadays, but I prefer it and wish I'd done it years ago.

The table is set for four. Jarvis's ma comes to stay one night a week in my old room, and I look forward to it. At his insistence my father now has a cosy little room we renovated from a disused barn next to the workshop.

"A man and wife need privacy, lass, this will do me nicely," he told me, "What more creature comforts does a man want than a bed, a fire and a homecooked meal?"

Not before time Liam will marry Sarah on 5th April next year. I'm to be matron-of-honour and Jarvis will be best man, and we couldn't be happier that they will finally get the chance to start their new life.

Da's long wait to know his fate finally ended when the coroner concluded the inquest into Ferguson's death with a verdict of lawful killing. Jarvis's statement that da acted in self-defence was the key evidence and the police confirmed they would not be pressing charges.

As for my mother, the same coroner ruled unlawful killing by a person or persons unknown. The police said they believed the perpetrator had fled the country and they were winding down the investigation. However, Jarvis later confided that Mr Douglas never gave up hope of finding some independent evidence that could bring Walter Davies to justice for her death. He said she deserved that.

Now it's the end of November the nights are drawing in. I always give the cottage a good bottoming on a Thursday, not because ma comes to pick fault with the standard of my housekeeping, I just like it to be nice for her staying with us. Along with her son she's made a fine start patching and mending my broken heart.

It was last New Year's Eve when everything changed.

Jarvis had been visiting every day since Boxing Day and that night on the stroke of midnight he went outside to bring a piece of coal inside for luck. We sang *Auld Lang Syne* then Jarvis turned to my father with a serious expression.

"I wonder if you would do me the great honour of granting your blessing in me marrying your daughter, sir?" he asked.

My father had downed a couple of whiskies by then and was looking rosy cheeked and relaxed in his best shirt and the jumper I'd knitted him a few Christmases ago.

"By heck, I thought you were never going to ask, lad," he said, "but you can cut out the 'sir' nonsense. Charlie will do nicely from now on."

It was the best start to the year I could ever have wished for, the bleakness of January I'd been so worried about just disappeared after that one little question.

The wedding was just us and the Morton's. My father trimmed the cart with white ribbon and Bella took us to church. I made my dress from white cotton and lace embroidered with yellow roses, my mother's favourite.

"Be happy, Pippin," my father whispered in my ear before he walked me down the aisle in his suit, a yellow rose from our own rose bush pinned to his lapel, "I sense there's somebody else by your side today."

Each step I took down the aisle towards Jarvis the more at peace I felt. Love was weaving its unspoken magic all around us in that quiet little church.

But it was after we stepped out of the church that we had our biggest surprise. The whole village barring one or two, had turned out to shower us with rice and good wishes. There was a sea of faces beaming our way in the sunshine, all there to wish us well in our new life.

I shall never forget that moment. It was the moment I finally felt accepted, part of the wider community. Strangely, I wasn't shy for the first time with all eyes upon me.

Then after a little fuddle in the back room of the *Rose & Crown* I snuck away early to go back to the cottage with my new husband. My father was staying away for the night in the room they let out over the pub, so we could have the house to ourselves.

Jarvis lifted me off my feet to carry me over the threshold, his face all serious and earnest until he tripped over the mat, and we collapsed in fits of giggles.

""I would rather be happy than dignified,"" I said, taking off my bonnet and quoting the line from *Jane Eyre.*

"I think it was about halfway through that book that I realised what I felt for you was love," he said, circling me in his arms.

We fell into a kiss—our first proper kiss as husband and wife—and my own love awakened except this time in a new and special way. The cottage was ours alone and a wonderful freeing sensation washed over me as our kiss turned into something more. I knew what was happening, but the feeling it aroused in me was newfound.

"Pip, what are you doing to me; I need you right now, will you have me? I can wait until tonight if this is not what you imagined."

My mouth in his neck I whispered, "We've waited so long and even now this is so much more than I ever imagined."

He felt powerful, and I knew then what I wanted.

We went upstairs to our new room. The room where I'd worked hard to lay the ghosts to rest so it could be ours. My father had made us an exquisite new bed as a wedding gift, and I'd lovingly made a quilt over the winter months. I'd got ready for my wedding in there that morning, and I knew then the room had finally become our own.

Jarvis unbuttoned my dress and slipped it from my shoulders. My chemise and underskirt followed quickly so I was stood before him, full sunlight streaming on my body, yet I felt no shyness whatsoever.

"Oh, Pip, my beautiful girl," he moaned laying me on the bed. I spread my arms above my head as I watched him take off his clothes, enjoying what was mine and all mine for the taking. His eyes never straying from mine, I could see the passion, the longing looking back at me and when he pushed himself inside me, I cried out with a ferocious mixture of pain and pleasure making him stop and stroke my hair.

"I can stop if it's too much," he whispered.

"No," I said in almost a wail, "don't stop, I don't want you to."

I could not believe that person was me, that person was coy, awkward Pip. Something had changed me, so I didn't feel shame at saying words that came from a place I didn't understand, not then. They overtook my being.

His love gained momentum until it poured into me making us both cry out with the release. My head was swimming, my legs shaking as he whispered into my hair how much he loved me, how this was so much more than any feeling he'd ever had. He explained perfectly what was running through my mind and when we kissed, my world had shifted.

My love had come home.

Nothing more, nothing less.

*

"My dear girl, this looks delicious, you spoil us, you really do," ma says now, daintily cutting into her pie, while Jarvis and my father tuck in. They nod, seeking to confirm the compliment.

Jarvis catches my eye. We speak without words, our love running quiet and deep, so words are often unnecessary.

"Have you said yes yet to the big job?" Jarvis asks.

My father finishes his mouthful and looks him straight in the eye.

"The question is, son: are you up to it?"

Jarvis smiles. I know what he's thinking—my father's no-nonsense approach is the quality he admires most about him.

"Yes, I think I am. Over nine months of intensive apprenticing has made me ready I'd say. What does Liam think?"

My father gives a low chuckle.

"Well, don't get too big for your boots, but he's glad you're onboard and we can take on more work. It will be you and him in a few years, I'll have to take a backseat and I might start doing it before too long. Two's company, three's a crowd sometimes."

"Whoa there," Jarvis says, "I'll not run until I can walk properly."

We laugh. Laughter has eluded this cottage for so many years. Even before my mother left it was heavy with tension because she was carrying so much on her shoulders. Far more even than we realised it turns out.

Ma puts her hand on Jarvis's forearm, so he looks her way.

"Policeman or no, your dad would be proud of what you've done with your life, lad," she says.

Tears sting my eyes. I know he was sure of his change of direction for himself, but this affirmation from his mother will be the seal.

"You're getting sentimental in your old age ma, I think," he says, but the expression in his eyes is telling her a different story.

By nine o'clock my father has wandered off to his little cabin as he calls it, and ma is in bed upstairs. I send Jarvis up with our hot milk, telling him I won't be long.

"What are you up to?" he asks mugs in hand at the foot of the stairs.

"Never you mind," I tell him with a smile.

"Do what you must then get yourself upstairs woman," he says with a twinkle in his eye.

Oh gladly, I think.

As I listen to each familiar creak of the stairs, I head to the drawer in the kitchen table my father made when he first came to live here with his first wife, Peggy all those years ago. I try not to think of the pain he's been through since, losing two wives and our baby brother, Isaac. Nobody deserves the peace he has finally found more. The sadness still sits behind his eyes but it's lessening, and I hope very soon it will lessen even more.

This little draw holds random kitchen paraphernalia, and I can be sure nobody else goes in it. I pull out a neatly folded piece of paper. The note is folded inside the book of words I wrote after my mother left so I wouldn't ever forget them. I'll be forever grateful she left her books behind as I feel like she's still here, hidden in every passage. I wonder if that was her intention because I know her books were her friends.

Unlike Jarvis, I'm far better with the written than the spoken word and I'd like to tell my husband he is to become a father in the most memorable way I can. My eyes scan the words now, satisfied I've told him exactly what it means to me to be able to give us a new generation to hold dear. To be the mother my own mother was despite the demons of her past catching up with her. I press the love-filled note to my chest and hold it to me a moment, so many thoughts racing through my mind I must close my eyes.

I've been thinking about my mother and father as parents more than ever of late since I discovered I was to have a baby. I imagine being pregnant does that to you, makes you look back and reflect on your childhood.

To me he will always be my da. He's put me before himself and made sure I had everything I could ever want and need, loved me with his whole heart like every good parent should. I am of his blood in the true sense, there's no doubt about it.

So, I don't blame him for lying to me about my mother losing the baby when she came to England. He only lied to protect me and I'm sure now I would have done the very same.

I know who my birth father is, in the eyes of the law at least. I saw it in his eyes that day I went to see my mother in that hovel of a house they shared, and he appeared like a dark shadow looming over me. I am determined to be free of the darkness after tonight.

That day, it wasn't just his evil I wanted to bolt from, it was the realisation of something I didn't understand then.

I understand it now, like I understand my mother died of a broken heart and Brendan Ferguson, was the man who broke it.

Enough, Pip I scold myself as I pick up the candle and put the love note in my dress pocket. Instead, I turn my thoughts to Jarvis waiting upstairs for me in our bed.

My mother had a difficult relationship with her father and perhaps that was some of the problem when it first came to choosing a husband. She told me the long-held notion is that without knowing it most girls end up marrying a man like their father. But if this is the case, you must make sure you admire him, or you'll live to regret it. In the end it seems she finally found her true father figure in my da, and he saved her for as long as she let him.

Perhaps I put you on a pedestal, mam, perhaps you weren't right about everything but on this occasion, your advice was spot on.

Jarvis is so like my da.

And I swear I couldn't love him any more than I do because of it.

Epilogue
1870 - Orla & Charlie

This is the first time Charlie Metcalfe has stepped foot over the threshold in six and a half days. He's lying in the long grass, chewing a dried stem and watching the clouds roll by. Only minutes ago, they were being elusive, but now they've swarmed like bees meaning rain isn't far behind. If only he could be one of those clouds, he thinks pulling a fresh stem of grass, all this turmoil would be over.

He has tried his best to keep going. After his parents died, he found his place living out here in the wilderness. He had his wife, his tools and his home in that order, and that was all he wanted.

But that was before.

Two years is long enough to grieve. That was the mantra he'd been telling himself until six days ago. Then on that day he suddenly didn't believe his mantra any longer. That day he decided to stay in bed, then the next day and the next, until today when he had an overpowering feeling he's still unable to describe.

He's a sensible man but it was strong enough to make him get up, bathe in the stream and put on clean clothes. His hair is combed, his teeth have been cleaned with soot and salt and now he's lying here. He's not sure how he got here but he's already glad he did.

Charlie's eyes are lolling, and a peaceful nap beckons. He may have taken to his bed, but sleep was fitful and sparse. He laid awake but he never cried once.

His eyes are still heavy but now they're trying to open of their own accord with a struggle.

There seems to be a girl looking down on him, but it's not Peggy. This girl has pale skin and blue eyes, dark hair hanging about her shoulders. It must be a dream because he doesn't know her at all. Peggy's hair was light brown and always in a bun unless she was in bed and then she wore it in a plait.

The girl turns to walk away and suddenly Charlie bends from the waist to sit bolt upright, the stem of grass falling from his lips.

"Stop, don't go," he shouts too loudly so the girl spins around with a frightened look on her face. Charlie is uncertain if the girl is still only living in his dream.

"I'm sorry, I didn't want to wake you," she says in an accent different to any other he's heard before. She's backing away as she speaks, her dress lifted above her knees to navigate her way through the long grass.

The tables turn suddenly and now he's the one who's alarmed when she trips and falls backwards with a short scream. Charlie is up and running before he even has time to think.

She's real, she's here, he's sure of it now.

Her chest is heaving from shock, but then his eyes lower to her stomach. It sits proud, pushing against the cotton of her dress.

He drops to the floor to sit cross-legged by her side apologising, asking if she's hurt and if he can help her up all at once.

"In a minute," she says, turning her head to look at him, "I'll just get my breath if you don't mind."

"Of course not," Charlie says, "take all the time you need."

Stretching his legs out in front of him he leans back with his hands on the grass behind him. He lifts his face to the dappling sunshine, and they sit together like this for some time.

"I've been to see those unmarked soldiers' graves," the girl says, "I came across them on my Sunday walk a few weeks ago and I've been out every Sunday since."

He sits forward, grasping his ankles and turns to look at her face. He deliberately avoids his eyes straying to her swollen stomach.

Where did she come from; who is she married to? So many questions are forming already about this young woman.

"It's a while since I noticed the graves," Charlie says, "I've had a lot on my mind."

There was no pause before he said the last part of his statement. This is unlike him, he's a man who ordinarily would never unload his troubles to anyone, let alone a stranger. Oddly, he has no regrets, no desire to take the words back.

"I can tell," she says.

He waits for her to continue, but she doesn't, and he doesn't push her for more.

"I've named each soldier and I've given them all a backstory. I thought it only right somebody should."

Yes, somebody should, Charlie agrees, and he would very much like to hear a tale of a fallen soldier.

"Which story is your favourite?" he asks.

She looks up at the sky for a moment considering her answer while he studies her white skin and dark lashes. Her hair is now fanned around her face in the flattened grass.

"George Duncan's story is my favourite," she concludes, "George was engaged to a girl called Aria from Scotland and she was waiting for him to come home from the battles. But he never returned.

Aria loved George so much she never married because every man after him would fall short. Aria was not prepared to waste her life on a man who was second-best."

Oh, he wasn't expecting such a story. The girl has clearly given it so much thought to offer the layering of detail and emotion.

"Your story is beautiful, but sad," he says, deciding on the truth, "may I ask your name?"

"You may. My name is Orla and I'm from a place called County Donegal in Ireland. I'm staying in the village with Mrs. Brownlow for a while."

This girl is alone in the world, he thinks. This girl was sent to him today for a reason he realises, and he will not ignore it.

"I'm Charlie. My cottage isn't far from here, would you like to join me for a glass of apple juice in the garden?"

Orla lifts up her forefinger and though he stares at it he's not taken aback. She traces her finger slowly around his eyes, down the bridge of his nose and then finally draws an outline around his lips. Charlie sits perfectly still all the while she does it, then when she drops her hand, they offer each other a shy smile.

The rain never came that day.

That was the day Orla went with Charlie to his cottage for the first time. Not long afterwards they were married, and she never wanted to be anywhere else again. They raised a family together and lived happily ever after.

That was until the day Orla Metcalfe packed her bags and ran away.